Trapped In Paradise

By Kenneth
D. MacHarg

Global Village Press

Carrollton, Georgia USA

Copyright © 2023 Kenneth D. MacHarg. All rights reserved. No part of this publication may be reproduced in any form or by any means, electronic or mechanical, including photocopying, recording, or by an information storage and retrieval system—except by a reviewer who may quote brief passages in a review to be printed in a magazine, newspaper, or on the web or by others wishing to use brief quotes or references in other works—without permission in writing from the author.

Other books by Kenneth D. MacHarg:

- *Tune in the World, The Listener's Guide to International Shortwave Radio*, Miller Publishing Company, Media, Pennsylvania, 1983
- *Introducing International Radio,* Global Village Press, Jeffersonville, In, 1987
- *A Haven By The Side Of The Road, The Story of Wayside Christian Mission*, Wayside Christian Mission, Louisville, Kentucky, 1997
- *Don't Rush the Lord, A Pilgrimage to God's Purpose*, Wm. Carey Library, Pasadena, California, 1997
- *Inside Track: Latin America Through the Eyes of a Missionary Journalist,* Editorial Buena Semilla, Bogotá, Colombia, 2001
- *Proclaiming the Gospel; Guidelines for Local Christian Radio Programming Around the World,* Latin America Mission, Miami, Florida, 2003. Published in Spanish as: *La proclamación del Evangelio; Pautas para programadores locales de radio cristiana alrededor del mundo,* Latin America Mission, Miami, Florida, 2003 and in Portuguese as: *Proclamando o Evangelho no rádio,* Transcultural Editora e Livraria Ltda., Anápolis, Brazil. 2004
- *Not in Vain*, with David M. Howard, Latin America Mission, Miami, Florida, 2005. *Also available in Spanish*
- *From Rio to the Rio Grande; Challenges and Opportunities in Latin America,* Global Village Press, Miami, Florida 2007
- *Radio Survives and Thrives, The History of Kentucky Broadcasting from 1945-1970,* Global Village Press, Carrollton, Georgia 2011
- *Singing the Lord's Songs in a Foreign Land; Biblical Reflections for Expatriates,* Global Village Press, Carrollton, Georgia, 2011
- *From Bangkok to Bishkek, Budapest to Bogota, The Compelling Story of International Congregations,* EnerPower Press, Gonzolaz, Florida, 2020

Chapter 1

It was the silence that woke him up.

David's eyes popped open and he became alert. Almost as quickly, he realized that the usual ambient noises were gone. The air conditioner, the refrigerator, the overhead fan, all had stopped—the victims of another *Apagón*—a power outage.

He had lived long enough in the tropics to recognize the symptoms of a night-time interruption to the power supply. There was the sudden silence, the darker-than-usual ambiance, the almost immediate slight increase in the temperature and the humidity level. Nevertheless, every time it happened, he would be startled awake for a few minutes until his brain clicked in and helped him recognize what had happened. Then, he usually rolled over and dropped back into sleep.

David and Alicia had spent most of their married life as global nomads. After college at a small school in Tennessee and doctoral studies in Kentucky (his in international relations and business, hers in language studies), they sought employment overseas and had spent the intervening time teaching in such far-flung places as Ecuador, Thailand, Bahrain, South

Africa and others before settling in Costa Brava five years previously.

They were true expats; third-culture people who no longer felt at home in American society nor ever really became a part of the society in the countries where they lived.

Where they felt most comfortable was among expatriates—Brits, Americans, South Africans, Dutch—people like themselves who spent most of their time living abroad and knew expat society and issues better than those of their native lands.

They barely understood U.S. politics anymore, and they followed local Costa Bravan politics only because the manipulations of corruption, power structures and the love-hate relationship with their homeland could come to affect them by surprise if they didn't pay attention.

They had lived through a political coup in one country, a major earthquake in another and ugly anti-American riots in a third where the U.S. military rescued them with barely the clothes on their backs. Just getting caught in traffic jams from anti-government riots or without transportation to work because of a bus strike could disrupt their whole day if they didn't pay attention.

So, they followed North American and local events a bit. But what they could really discuss were issues such as the intricacies of U.S. tax exemptions for people living overseas, local changes in visa requirements, which U.S. universities were most open to expat, third-culture children and whether a new shipment of Cheerios, peanut butter and Dr. Pepper had arrived at the *MegaBodega* supermarket.

Wanderlust had moved David and Alicia from spot to spot for over thirty years. There is something about the expat life that makes people restless. Whether they like their situation or not, every three to five years they felt the need or desire to relocate, even if it was just to a new apartment. So, they had done just that; Asia, Africa, Latin America, Europe, the Middle East—they had spent at least a few years in each of those regions. And, each time they had felt the need to move on.

Costa Brava was different, however. Maybe age was creeping up on them or the adjustment to a new culture, new people and new food was becoming more difficult. Perhaps they were growing weary of the constant changes. They had even begun to talk about which international retirement haven they should consider—Mexico where over a million Americans had settled was one. But they had also considered Mallorca along with one or two Caribbean islands, several towns along the Spanish Mediterranean coast and Thailand, a country they particularly liked.

But then they accepted a position at the university in Costa Brava and fell in love with the country. The warm, but not too humid, climate at 3,800 feet was very comfortable. The stability of government, proximity of both mountains and beaches and broad expat community made them feel very much at home.

For Alicia it also had the advantage of being only a few hours by air from both of their children. The oldest, Rich, lived with his wife in the Central American country of El Salvador where he was the country director for an NGO, a non-government organization. The younger of the two, Melanie, worked for an import-export company in Miami and passed through several times a year.

Both kids were typical expat children. In their adult lives they either lived internationally or worked for an international organization that provided the opportunity to travel overseas. And, typical of their breed, they also moved every few years.

David began to drift back to sleep when he suddenly woke up again. It sure was quiet. These *Apagones* were frequent and it was always quiet, but tonight is seemed even more so.

Normally during a blackout he could hear traffic on the nearby highway, the sirens of ambulances bringing the sick, injured and dying to the hospital across the valley, the occasional roar of a plane taking off from the international airport heading who knows where.

Of course, there were the natural sounds of some crickets, a few strange insect and bird calls, but none of the man-made sounds he was used to hearing.

Just then, Alicia groaned lightly as she shifted in bed.

David sighed and drifted back to sleep once again.

Chapter 2

Dawn comes early in the tropics. By five thirty a.m. the sun had totally cleared the horizon. David often thought that if the country would just shift one hour earlier, like daylight savings time, it would mesh better with the lives of people and save the country millions of dollars in electrical bills. After all, scientific research had demonstrated that in the average home, 25 percent of electric power was used for lighting and small appliances, such as TVs and stereos and a good percentage of that consumption occurred in the evening when families were home. By moving the clock ahead one hour, the amount of electricity consumed each day decreased. But such ideas were always rejected by the more conservative rural population that had to be up anyhow so enjoyed the daylight. And, besides, the later rising was reflective of the local population's vibrant and social natures that included late dining as well as long evening parties and dances.

But for city folks, it was a waste of precious daylight that could better be enjoyed in the evening after work. Other than laborers who began their work early, and the ever-increasing number of joggers on the streets, the public walks and streets of the city were never even close to filling up until well after six a.m. Some newspaper vendors didn't even show up on street corners until almost seven because there wasn't enough traffic earlier to warrant the bother.

David turned and looked over at the clock. Nothing. That was a surprise; the power hadn't come back on yet. He checked his watch—6:15. Time to get moving.

"Morning, Hon." He greeted her in his cheerful voice.

Alicia, as usual, was up first. How she could always be alert so early in the morning he could never figure out. It took him at least 30 minutes to be able to see more than three feet or to figure out what day it was.

"The power's out."

"Yeah, I know. It went out some time during the night. I don't know how long ago."

The outage meant that David wouldn't get his morning news fix. It was automatic, shuffle out to the kitchen, say hello, turn on the television, and settle in for the headlines.

Not that there was much on the news these days. The U.S. networks fed a daily diet of scandal, celebrity news and the political drama of the week. There might be one international headline among the mix, but only if it involved American policies or military action. What was that old adage, "coups and earthquakes?" That's all the overseas information that ever mattered to domestic networks. Why the local cable system didn't carry CNN International or the BBC he could never figure out.

The *apagón* would not unduly affect breakfast. Alicia had long-ago become accustomed to preparing meals on her one burner gas stove that they used for camping. In fact, she had turned out some excellent meals on that single burner over the years. David always marveled at how she did it. And, they both had learned how to open and close a refrigerator door quickly or not at all during power outages. It never made sense why manufacturers didn't make chest refrigerators the way they made chest freezers. Those would be so much more efficient: the cold air, since it settles, flows out of a stand-up refrigerator, reducing its efficiency. *"But who was going to listen to him?"* he thought letting out a soft sigh.

David decided not to worry about cable systems or appliance manufacturers or even *apagones*. Neither of them had classes scheduled for the day so they had planned to move slowly and go in a little late. He would just relax, eat breakfast, scan the newspaper, and they both would leave for the university around ten or eleven a.m.

With no television, David decided to fetch the paper. Even that often arrived late, sometimes not until after seven, but it was worth the trip down the stairs from their third-floor apartment.

Outside the door, he stopped suddenly. While the silence had woken him in the middle of the night, it was the absolute silence of the day that arrested his still-groggy attention. He listened—something was missing. Of course, the dull roar of air conditioning was absent, but there was something, or to be accurate, nothing else making even a bit of noise. Not one urban sound could be heard. No traffic, no sirens, no distant televisions or mechanical equipment, no motorcycles delivering newspapers, no school busses collecting children on their morning routes, no voices…nothing. Just dead silence.

Where were the beginnings of stirrings at the school across the street? It wouldn't be long until the yard was full of noisy children arriving. But there was no one there yet to even open the door or yard. And normally David and Alicia could smell whatever was being baked at the moment as the divine smells from what they called the "cookie factory" drifted across the valley. In fact, the plant baked all kinds of snacks and goodies and they had learned to identify the product of the day: cookies, crackers or snacks. But today there was no wonderful odor wafting into his nostrils, nor stirrings at the school.

David shuddered at the thought of no one around. He quickly shook off the queasy feeling he had and padded downstairs to see if the paper had arrived yet. No such luck…running late again.

Back upstairs, Alicia had turned out a few scrambled eggs, a piece of ham each, some Granny Toast that she also fried over the burner and a passable cup of coffee. If Costa Brava was famous for anything it was its coffee, and both of them, during their wanderings to and fro over the face of the earth, had come to be connoisseurs of the drink. But, nothing they had found was as good as the local bean of Costa Brava grown on the beautiful undulating mountainsides just outside of town. Often their morning coffee reminded them that the neighborhood where they now lived had been a vast coffee plantation just thirty years earlier. Those thoughts always led to their memories of the emerald green acres of coffee bushes, laden with the red berries that would someday be someone's morning cuppa joe.

After a leisurely breakfast, made tense only by their unspoken uneasiness about the extended outage, David announced that he was going to walk up to the corner grocery store or perhaps the several blocks to the neighborhood mall where the large *MegaBodega* grocery chain had one of their super stores. "I just need to see if anybody has any information on the power outage," he explained. "I'll be right back."

David enjoyed morning walks in the city. Compared to the highly polluted downtown area, the suburban streets of San Juan were relatively fresh, though often littered with trash as dogs might have invaded and scattered it as it waited to be picked up by the garbage collectors. A stroll through the neighborhoods where houses were fringed with flowers, bougainvillea spilled over walls and birds twittered away in the trees always gave him a lift and helped to stretch out his cramped legs.

The *apagón* must have made everyone late he mused as he crested the slight rise and rounded the corner onto the nearest main street. Nobody was on the streets, and, disturbingly, David discovered that there were no cars operating anywhere.

Picking up his step, he came to the local corner store where he and Alicia usually stopped for bread, milk, soft drinks and whatever they needed to pick up on the way home. It was closed; unusual for this time of the morning.

Then he saw the first of what would become an overwhelming number of similar discoveries. There, on the corner, around the side of the little mini store lay the body of Mauricio, the night watchman.

Chapter 3

David drew a quick breath and stepped back. Quickly he looked around but could find nothing else out of the ordinary. His eyes were drawn back to the very still corpse of the semi-uniformed guard. His body showed no signs of violence or injury. For that David was glad. They had exchanged pleasantries almost every morning for five years. He was an affable enough chap, and the shock of seeing his lifeless body sent yet another strong chill up his back.

Quickly he stepped away and began to walk rapidly to the mall. Two blocks later he came across the next body…that of a homeless man who often slept wrapped in a cardboard box under the overhang of a store. At first David was a bit relieved…he probably was sleeping, and maybe he hadn't looked close enough at the guard…perhaps he had been asleep too.

But, David stepped close and checked—no breathing. He shook the homeless man gently at first, then with increasing violence. No response. He turned the body over, and the man's arm flopped down onto the pavement. Dead!

David ran the rest of the way to the *MegaBodega* store at the mall. It was open 24-hours a day. Surely there would be someone there who could assure him that things were or would return to normal.

There was dead silence in the mall. David shuddered again as that thought passed his cerebrum. It was dark inside—either the big industrial generators that most stores and businesses had because of the frequent power outages hadn't kicked on when the power went out, or they had already run out of fuel. Inside it appeared there was no one alive. Then, as he entered the *MegaBodega* he came to an abrupt halt. In the dimness of the building, illuminated by filtered light coming through a few skylights, he saw two young cashiers sprawled over the checkout counters...dead, just like the others. A quick sweep through the store uncovered three deceased customers as well as a few other employees who had been stocking shelves. They were all spread out with no visible signs of what took their lives, but each with an unusually peaceful expression on their face.

David reached for his cell phone and tried to dial home. No dial tone; the service was out.

He panicked. Grabbing a few items (he wasn't sure until later why: milk, bread, a cooked chicken, some fruits and vegetables, a package of cookies and a few bottles of drinking water. He ran from the store, planning to go back and pay later, and made his way down the hill to the house.

Running up the stairs, he burst into the apartment and double locked the door behind him.

"Alicia!" he screamed.

She appeared out of the bathroom, her hair wrapped in a towel. "What on earth is the matter?"

she queried. "Why are you rushing in here, slamming the door and yelling at me in a wild panic?"

He momentarily stopped short. *Why hadn't she sensed the same silence as he had? Why was she nonchalantly just getting out of the shower?* Ignoring that for the moment, his words tumbled out.

"They're dead, they're all dead!" David could barely blurt out his words. Panic choked his voice, his body shook uncontrollably. His usually analytical mind was racing so fast and so far that he couldn't put anything together.

"Who's dead?" Alicia asked. "Calm down, stop shaking and make some sense."

David collapsed into one of the dining room chairs. "They're dead. Everybody…guards, cashiers, stock boys, customers…they're all dead."

Alicia sat down in a chair opposite David and drew a deep breath. "All right, now slow down and tell me what's going on. What did you see? Which guards and cashiers are dead? Who else is out and around? What are the police doing?"

"There aren't any police; no one is out and around and there is no traffic at all. No cars, no buses, no trucks, no motorcycles. There aren't any pedestrians or joggers. There is nobody out there; at least nobody who is alive. I was the only person from here to the mall who was alive and walking."

David took a breath. "The guard at the ministore at the corner, Mauricio, the guy I say hi to every morning? He's dead and the store is closed. The homeless guy outside the store up the block? He's not sleeping, he's dead. And at the *MegaBodega,* nobody is alive. The cashiers, the guard, the guys stocking the shelves, a few customers, they're all dead. Dead as a doornail. I checked them. Dead!"

The room fell silent. Outside the couple could hear a parrot chattering away, a twittering bird and somewhere in the distance they began to hear a howling dog. Both of them felt a strange chill as the dog lifted its howl to the unusually clear, sunlit sky.

"Let me get this right," she said softly. "Outside there is no traffic, not even a bicycle?"

"Right."

"Nobody out walking, no joggers, *nadie*?"

"Right again."

"And, every human being that you saw, from here to the corner and on up to the *MegaBodega* and back...every human being was...dead?"

"Right. And, not only that, the power is out all over the neighborhood, the generators at the mall aren't running, and, this is the scary part, there is absolutely no human sound. None of the sounds of the city that you would expect...no cars, no horns, no sirens, no buses, no air conditioning, no generators, no police whistles, nothing, *nada*!"

Alicia began to tremble and then to cry softly. "There must be some reason for this." Suddenly she jumped up and slammed shut the big front window that she opened each morning when she got up. "Maybe it's some sort of poisoning, some sort of gas escape, you know, like Bhopal," she said.

"Yeah, I thought of that," David agreed. "Maybe so, but, if that's the case, why aren't we dead? Our apartment isn't airtight. We should be dead, too.

I thought about that when I was outside, but I didn't smell or sense anything and...there are animals and birds alive all around us. I saw a few dogs on the street just wandering like always. And, you can hear dogs and birds outside right now. If it was a chemical leak, you would think that they would have been killed as well."

Alicia thought for a moment. "Well, maybe it's something that just affects humans and not animal life. That doesn't sound very logical, but who knows. Who knows what's happening, how far widespread it is, what it is, who is affected, who will be affected."

"The radio!" David sprang up and sprinted to the bedroom. He and Alicia had started their worldwide wanderlust in the days long before international satellites, CNN or the internet. Now, even with the accessibility of new communication technologies, David had kept his old World Master shortwave radio...and it was battery powered.

He fit the earphones over his head and turned on the radio. A quick scan across the FM band brought the hiss of vacant frequencies from static, picked up by the batteries. "The local FM stations are off the air," he shouted to Alicia.

Over to the AM band. Even in the morning it should bring in some stations from out of town, even one or two from neighboring countries. Nothing. "Reception conditions aren't good today," he shouted, keeping to himself a growing fear and doubt that anything was on the air.

Hesitantly, he switched to the shortwave bands, hoping to at least find an international frequency station such as the BBC from London, The Voice of America from Washington or others that could be heard from around the world. He pushed some of the buttons for the pre-tuned stations he had entered. Silence.

Panicked, he started scanning the bands, 15 meters, 19 meters—good frequencies for the morning hours. He heard nothing. On to 25, 31, 49 meters, nighttime frequencies but with some regional daytime possibilities. Again, he heard nothing, no stations, no automated "sweepers" that passed through the bands detecting unusual earthly signals or extraterrestrial sounds or code.

Slowly he went back to the table and slumped into the chair.

"Well?"

"Hon, do you remember the *War of the Worlds*—that old radio program that fooled many people into thinking that the world had been invaded by martians?

Alicia shuddered. "Well, yeah, I heard it once—at a Halloween party."

"Yeah, well…do you remember how it ended?"

"No, not exactly…well, everybody died…except a few, right?"

"Right. Look, I scanned the FM, AM and shortwave bands. There was nothing, *nada*, zilch. I'll check tonight, when the reception is better, but, I'm not sure what's going on here, or anywhere. I was hoping I would hear something, but unless some force has blocked radio and electronic waves at the same time, it may have killed a whole lot of people...I'm really scared."

He paused and drew a deep breath. "Do you remember exactly how the War of the Worlds radio program ended?"

Alicia shook her head no.

"It ended with a ham radio operator trying to contact somebody, anybody. I remember his voice, '2X2L...calling CQ 2X2L....calling CQ... calling 8X3R...coming back at 2X2L.' And, the original operator responded, 'How's reception? How's reception? Where are you, 8X3R? What's the matter? Where are you?"

"So?" Alicia's voice trembled.

"David was silent for a long time. "8X3R never answered back," he said. "I was hoping to at least hear something like 2X2L calling CQ, 2X2L calling CQ, but there was just plain nothing."

Chapter 4

It was the longest day that they could remember. Soon after the unsuccessful radio scan, Alicia got up and closed the front blinds. The darkness of the room made things seem even more ominous, but both thought that while they longed to see another human being, just one, alive, it was best to hide their presence from whatever force or being there might be wandering, if any.

From time to time one or the other would peek out between the slats to see if there was any sign of life. For an hour late in the morning black smoke rose from one spot on the other side of the city, but it soon went away.

Alicia put together a light lunch and they both ate in silence, both ambient and their own. Early in the afternoon, David thought he saw a flash of light from the side of one of the mountains, but soon realized it was just the afternoon sun bouncing off one of the thousands of tin-roofed homes that dotted the mountainside.

By mid-afternoon he decided to risk the possibility of an appearance and went out on the balcony for a quick scan of the neighborhood and the city skyline. Using his binoculars, he checked out nearby homes. There wasn't any life or movement. The *autopista*, empty of the usual cars and trucks this time of day, was barely visible through the trees. He perused whatever streets he could see, the windows of distant skyscrapers, and the mountain ridges surrounding the city.

There was nothing moving, and the absolute silence of the large urban area became so oppressive and frightening that he retreated into the apartment, double-locking the door behind him, though he was already beginning to wonder about the need to do so. But, habits die hard, and it is so customary to lock doors behind you in many countries.

The couple's cat settled in his lap, purring and oblivious to what was happening, or more correctly, *not* happening around them. David stroked her fur absentmindedly. "The next big step is the night," he said, almost to no one.

"What do you mean?"

"Oh, two things; First, with the night we will be able to tell if there are any lights in the city or up the mountainsides. Any kind of light; electric lights, a kerosene lantern, a flashlight, a candle, car lights, a fire, any kind of light."

"Well, yes, but will we be able to see small lights?" Alicia asked with doubt in her voice.

"Very likely," David responded. "I remember my parents talking about the blackouts during World War II along the east coast. Windows had to be sealed shut because even a small candle could be seen in the middle of a darkened city by approaching enemy bombers. And, if you were going to listen to the radio, you had to put a blanket over it."

"A blanket? Why?"

"Remember, those were tube radios and they usually had dial lights. Even the glow of a radio tube or that dim dial light could be seen in total darkness."

"Ok, what's the second thing about the night? You said two things."

"The radio. Reception is always better after dark. If, and I mean if, there are any kinds of radio stations on the air anywhere on AM or shortwave we should be able to hear them. You can even tune in some U.S. AM stations here at night if nobody else is on the same frequency. We'll see."

Alicia didn't respond. She and David spent the afternoon sitting, pondering, praying, and trying to read. The hours crept by. And their nerves remained on edge.

Because darkness comes quickly in the tropics, as does the dawn, they ate their dinner early. Again, it was a light meal because neither of them was particularly hungry. They ate more out of habit than of need.

The curtain of darkness dropped, as anticipated, right around 6 p.m. Anxious for the night, David opened the blinds early, wanting to see what happened, and sat back on the sofa which was the place to get the best view out the huge sliding windows.

They had enjoyed the view of the city and the mountains at sunset hundreds of times. Out their window the beautiful metropolis spread from one mountain range to the other. As night fell, lights would routinely pop on here and there, twinkling in the haze that hung over this somewhat humid city.

They never regretted the little extra rent to be on the third floor of the four-plex apartment building. Alicia and David selected it for the spectacular views, day or night. With a valley and rushing stream below, the view was obscured only slightly by the school. They were on the third floor and the school had only one level. Right now they were especially glad for the panorama.

Normally, rows of street lights lined winding roads in the valley and up the mountainside. Billboards and neon signs blinked their messages for passing motorists and those with a view. Eventually, as darkness fell, whole *urbanizaciones* (neighborhoods) would come alight along with sports fields, distant towns and scattered homes on the mountainside. On clear nights, which didn't happen too often, they could pick out the blinking lights of the broadcast towers atop Izkatzú, the towering volcano that dominated the valley.

This night, they sat with anxiety and anticipation, watching for the familiar warm glow of urban lighting that dominated the panorama, yet afraid of what they might or might not see.

The setting sun cast an orange glow on the mountains, reflecting off of the clouds that sat like a mantle on their peaks. Below, the lush green flanks turned a darker green, and then black as the sunset's rays climbed the mountainsides.

Alicia took David's hand as they watched the darkness fall. Here and there the spark of light from the last of the sun's rays against a window, a tin roof or a car's windshield gave them a moment of hope that somewhere, someone had turned on a light.

But, as the last light of day disappeared from behind them, they looked out across a valley as dark as any remote, uninhabited valley could be. Nowhere, in any direction, could they see even a hint of a light, the glow of a fire or cook stove being used in lieu of electric ovens, or the glance of the headlights of a car as it turned a corner or made its way around a curve.

On this moonless night, the valley and its surrounding mountainside were completely, absolutely dark. Other than the houses nearest to them or the outline of a multi-story apartment building against the ever-dimming sky, no sign of human habitation was visible.

It was as if they were the first people to come over the crest of a hill on the edge of the valley and look across at a vast, uninhabited landscape of trees, hills, mountains and valleys.

It was then that darkness began to take over them--a different kind of darkness brought on as hope of other human life faded. An awareness that they might be alone created chills and an overwhelming tension in them.

They did not want to give up hope quite yet, but it was becoming more and more the reality that was sinking in.

David picked up the World Master radio and turned it on. Slowly, almost afraid of what he *wouldn't* hear, he tuned the dial, first across the local FM band, then across the AM band, slowly, stopping on known frequencies of clear channel stations from North

America, and then across the many international broadcast and amateur bands.

From time to time he would stop and re-tune, thinking that maybe, just maybe, he had heard some faint signal, a note of music, a spoken word in whatever language, *any* language. He twisted the dial for several long minutes. Then, he turned the radio off and put down the earphones.

Alicia cried while David tightened his grip on her hand. Their worst, unspoken fears seemed to be all too real now. From all appearances, they just might be the only people alive in the city, in the region or…he drew a breath…in the world.

Chapter 5

"I never thought I would become a looter."

Alicia had just come into the kitchen to put together breakfast and was surprised to find David at the table scrawling furiously on a legal pad and mumbling to himself.

"What did you say?"

"Oh, hi Hon, I was just saying that I never thought I would become a looter."

Alicia blinked and looked at her watch. It was unusual to find David up, let alone doing anything constructive, before she awoke.

"But, this morning David had been awake before dawn, his mind charging, his creative juices running at top speed. They had slept some, much to their own surprise after such a stressful day yesterday. However, he had been up several times during the night, partially thinking and reflecting and reacting to the events of the previous day, partially to check one more time out the window to see if there were any lights anywhere.

As soon as it got light enough to see what he was writing, he started to make lists on his pad.

"What are you working on," Alicia asked, slowly tensing, beginning to register the trauma of the day before.

"Well, it looks like, as they say, we have a situation here. So, we need to organize ourselves, set some priorities and start gathering some stuff. That's why I'm talking about looting! If we are going to stock up on supplies, I'm essentially going to go to the store and…" He started to say steal, but couldn't bring himself to do it. "And…take them."

Alicia suppressed a giggle in what was not a humorous situation at all. "My university professor husband, former secret agent with top-level security clearance for governmental agencies, upstanding churchman is going to become a looter?"

David grinned, but then grew serious again." I guess so, but the reality is, we need to stock up on some supplies just in case this whole nightmare doesn't turn out to be just a bad dream brought on by eating too much pizza."

Alicia winced. She had been suppressing the reality of their experiences of the past 24 hours, and David's comment brought her back into touch with their predicament.

"Do we really need to stock up on stuff, as you call it? Can't we just go down to the *MegaBodega* and pick up things as we need them? We don't even know if this is a long term problem or if we only momentarily avoided the disaster of all those around us."

"I don't think we can go as we need things," David responded. His professionally trained mind had been mulling over all of the possibilities and options and he had come to some firm conclusions.

His analysis and planning was helped by his experiences a few years back providing consultation for several NGO development agencies, and a one-year rather clandestine, part-time stint as a strategic planner and advisor for the State Department during a time of unrest in a Middle Eastern country. That experience had taught him to consider all aspects of contingency planning and he had learned as much as he had taught to his employers. And, he was not one to take a lets-wait-and-see attitude, but rather a take-charge approach.

"One problem we have is that we don't know who else, if anyone, is alive here in San Juan, or in the country for that matter. Maybe no one else is alive, or maybe there are individuals, pockets of people or whole communities of people who survived this…this whatever."

He paused to let what he had said sink in for both of them.

"Well, if there were others, individuals or a whole bunch of people, what difference would that make?"

"That's just the question, we don't know what difference it would make. Maybe others would be fellow survivors who would band together to forge a new society and work for each other's well-being. Or, maybe, they would be just the opposite, panicked people driven to survive at any cost with no concern for others, people with a shoot first and don't bother to ask any questions later philosophy. And, desperate people like that *are* driven to looting and protecting themselves at any cost. So, while I want to be open, and am hoping and praying that there are others still alive here, we need to be doing what we need to, just in case. To at least provide for and protect ourselves for a couple of months until we get a handle on the larger picture.'

"Wow, I guess I hadn't thought about all of that." Alicia seemed stunned for a few moments. "First, I suppose, I just hoped this was all a bad dream where I would wake up this morning and everything would be back to normal. Second, I guess I'm just too trusting. I figured that anybody else alive would be just as glad to see us as we would be to see them."

"That's my hope too," David responded. "But, we have got to be prepared for any eventuality, and we have to at least take some steps to take care of ourselves in the short term until we figure out what is going on."

"Yeah, you're right. I'll put on the coffee. Tell me what you have written."

A few minutes later, David took his first sip of coffee (made on the camping burner) as Alicia settled down into her usual chair. They were, after almost 40 years of marriage, creatures of habit in many of their living patterns.

"OK, first, we need to stock up on food and essential supplies."

"Well, that sounds easy enough."

"On the one hand yes, on the other hand not necessarily so. Up at *MegaBodega* there is probably enough food to last us a year or more, if someone else doesn't take it all first or need it, for that matter."

David paused to reflect on how he had said that. He realized that his first thought was selfish, *me* first, *my* survival at all costs, and only secondarily did he consider that someone else might have equal needs and that he might, eventually, have to return to living and functioning in a society where the community good might surpass his own needs or desires.

He continued. "But there are limitations. Obviously the perishable goods will last only so long and some of them are probably already well on their way to being spoiled."

By now it had been over twenty-four hours since the electricity flow stopped and even closed freezers would hold food for only so long. Other coolers, where the milk, butter, cheese and other products were held may have already lost their cooling ability and the food may be on its way out in the warmer climate.

"Even canned goods have only so much shelf-life, though I think that we can count on several years for many of them," he said. "I don't know about packaged goods like beans, rice, flour, sugar and other instant-type foods. There is also the factor of bugs and mice in this climate."

Costa Brava had probably the most ideal climate anywhere. Ranging on the warm side year-round, there was no need for a heater though some at the higher elevations had space heaters along with their fireplaces. Nor was there really a need for air conditioning, though more and more residents, especially expats, had purchased them in recent years. David and Alicia would be spared the work to heat or cool themselves, lessening the burden of survival quite a bit.

"How is our fridge holding?"

"Fairly well, though I'm not too sure about some of the meat, nor the milk. If we can find ice that hasn't melted, I should cook the meat to make it last longer."

Alicia thought about the shopping they had done the past weekend when she had stocked up on beef and chicken for some upcoming dinner parties. If she didn't do something with the meat within the next day, she would have to throw it out, but even then she wasn't sure that she could store it well.

"OK." David's strategic juices were running again. "I think that the best thing to do is to take the Trooper to *MegaBodega* and back it up to the door and start loading, if it's not already wiped out."

David shuddered. His instincts told him that it would be just as he left it the day before, hanging open, several bodies, now beginning to deteriorate, throughout the store, and everything untouched, other than perhaps some of the meat which may have already been devoured by marauding dogs if they were clever enough to get into the refrigerators.

"The Trooper? Alicia sounded surprised and then relieved. "I had forgotten. Maybe we do have at least one creature comfort."

"Oh, we may have a few more that we can work out. But, for now, let's take one thing at a time."

Chapter 6

Before taking any further steps toward a new form of daily life and an adaptation to very changed circumstances, the couple first had the rather unpleasant task of removing the bodies of other residents in their apartment complex before they began to smell and become a health hazard.

By mutual agreement, the landlords who lived in the apartment below them, had exchanged keys with them, so David and Alicia were easily able to access the other apartment. The two brothers, of Indian descent, were affable chaps with whom they had carried on a wonderful relationship. Tending to their remains was, thus, difficult and emotional, but they were able to carry them to their Trooper and take them to a nearby graveyard where they found an already excavated site awaiting an anticipated burial. Placing them in the grave, they covered the bodies, stopped to pray and beat a hasty retreat back to their refuge at home. Fortunately, the other two apartments in the building were empty. One was vacant awaiting a potential new resident, and the occupant of the other was out of the country at the moment.

Stark and unpleasant thoughts of all the other bodies and what they were going to do with them before wild animals started to descend on the area looking for food began to penetrate their thinking. They remembered the night watchman and others

David had run across to this point. And there was a problem that needed to be considered…all were going to smell after a while as they decomposed.

The past twenty-four hours *had* been a nightmare. In fact, for both of them, it had been overwhelming and incomprehensible. To be faced with the possibility, no matter how remote, that they might be the only living human beings in the city, or the country or the world for that matter was beyond belief. That just went against everything and anything that they had experienced or thought about in their lives.

Compounding this for Alicia was the fact that she had not yet been any distance from the apartment, nor seen the bodies littered on the street. It was all a bit staggering the first time she saw it and she now understood why David had torn into the apartment in such shock. She was relatively calm as she listened to him yesterday, but now she had an entirely different point of view; one of consternation and repulsion. And her emotions began to get the best of her a couple of times as she helped carry the neighbor's bodies out to be buried.

They knew of major disasters or actions of war which had left communities decimated or whole nations vastly unpopulated. But, their experience of twenty-four hours in the middle of a city of one million with absolutely no sign of human life was mind-numbing, to say the least.

The enormity and personal loss of it all hadn't totally dawned on them yet. Partially because they were unable to deal with the possibility that they were all that was left, partially because they were in denial about any such possibility, and partially because their minds had been so preoccupied with other things that they had pushed such emotions aside.

Each of them had mentioned at least once a concern for their children, but again, they brushed the nagging anxiety aside and moved ahead. Since they could not hear any radio communication, possibly the kids had not survived either. But, neither wanted to face that fact yet.

The best thing seemed to keep moving and planning, leaving them little time to mull things over. Grieving could come later, and maybe by then they would know more about their circumstances and reality.

Once they had removed the bodies, the Trooper kicked over like any other car at any time. Alicia had breathed a sigh of relief. Just one thing that spoke of normality and the life she once knew meant something to her.

Now, with the car running, they were pulling away from the curb as on any other day.

No one could say that the car ran smoothly, but then, it never did. It was fifteen years old, had climbed many a mountain and forded multiple creeks and rivers. As a result, it had known better days. But, it was a four-wheel drive, and fulfilled their need for a car that would go almost anywhere, when it worked. Once it had dropped its gas tank on the way to work, creating quite a scene for those on the busy road.

The drive through the streets was very eerie. It was late morning and nobody, but nobody, was around. Here and there they saw a body on the sidewalk and had to swerve to miss some in the middle of the boulevard. Paper from trash blew with the wind and a few dogs were around scavenging through garbage. Otherwise, it was empty, strangely quiet, and frightening.

David backed the car up to the side entrance to the mall and tried to edge it up over the curb. That didn't work, so he let it go.

Slowly they got out and entered the silent center. Sunlight streamed through the overhead windows, reflecting off of the polished floor. Nothing moved, and the only life-like visions they captured were quick glances at mannequins in the display windows. Their hearts pounded as their footsteps echoed through the vacant building. They moved silently, concentrating on the task ahead, keeping a sharp eye and ear for any movement or unexpected sounds. There were none.

At the *MegaBodega* each of them grabbed one of the biggest shopping carts, pulling one body off to the side so they would be able to get the carts past it. And stepping around a few others near the door that appeared to David to be slightly swollen since yesterday. They began to move quickly through the aisles.

Alicia shivered at the thought of what she just did; pulled a person, a husband, brother, father off to one side, almost as if it was nothing more than a sack of cement that was in the way. Both of them dealt with strong emotions and thoughts, but tried to focus on the task at hand, and concentrate on what they would have to do to stay alive. It wasn't easy for either of them with the incident so recent.

In reality, David was slightly relieved not to see anybody at the mall. At least the goods would still be there, with no competition or possibility of violence over whatever they needed.

"Hon, we need to stock up on at least a month's worth of food and supplies," he directed. "Grab some bags from the check-out counter to load things into so we can save time and a step when we go to load the car. When you fill a cart, take it to the car and get another cart. We'll load it when we get a car-full. I'm going to load up several large bottles of water; you concentrate on food supplies, especially those that will last."

Each of them moved with focus and determination through the aisles, picking up dozens of bottles or cans of one product or another. David delivered three carts of water bottles to the car while Alicia cleaned out some of the supplies of vegetables and fruits, wondering how she could preserve them and wanting to make sure that should someone else come "shopping" she would have enough to sustain them for a while. She particularly concentrated on the coastal fruits, like pineapples and bananas, which did not grow in San Juan. She realized that there would not be anyone coming or going from the coast and that might be the last time they had them for a while, if ever again.

She found some of the frozen meat and vegetables still thawing deep in the freezer, so added them to a cart while grabbing a few picnic coolers to stuff them in. She wasn't so sure why she got so many, because with no electricity or generator they would only last for a short time. She mused, *Can we eat all these in a couple of days or will I throw them out?* But then she realized that they could try to eat them one way or another before they would rot. Or, she could preserve them in sealed jars if she could find the jars and the fuel to can them.

They even gathered a few treats—two cakes, several cartons of candy and a large bouquet of flowers which David would ceremoniously present to Alicia over a candle-light steak dinner later that day.

They decided on a half-gallon of ice cream, knowing they would likely make themselves sick eating the whole thing before it melted. They had grabbed one from deep down in the freezer to get the hardest one they could find.

What few things that were still good, would perish. Meat from the stores deep freeze would last a short while, but canned hams, tuna and salmon would last longer until they could solve the problem of food to sustain them for the long term.

They each grabbed certain products and items, based on their perspective. For Alicia, propane tanks for the stove, cleaning supplies, laundry soap, plastic tubs of the local dishwashing soap, as well as the food. For David, a few of the hardware items often stocked by a grocery store…tape, oil for the car, candles, batteries and flashlights.

At the car, they found they had gathered far more than they could fit in. Finally, before the day was over, they made four round-trips bringing home a myriad of food and supplies to get them through far more than a couple of weeks.

It was difficult to just walk off with all the loot, because they had seen such things on TV in various countries where there was civil unrest, and they condemned the participants. Now here they were doing it themselves. Guilt overcame them each at some point.

"Do you feel guilty doing something so opposed to our upbringing? I do," Alicia began.

"Yeah, I understand, but it is a matter of survival, and I guess that is the thing to think about now. Do you remember all our discussions about situation ethics?"

"Yes, but it is a little different thinking about a hypothetical game in a values clarification class and actually doing it..." Alicia trailed off in a soft voice.

They ended the conversation there and continued with the task at hand.

Emptying the store and carting it all up the stairs at the apartment or finding a storage place free of rain and animals was not quite so easy living on an upper floor. By the time they had filled the spare bedroom, the garage area down below and every available space, they were both exhausted. The hardest was lugging the coolers of the cold things and ice up to the apartment. With the emotional and physical toll they could hardly get up the stairs with the last load.

They collapsed on the sofa and just stared out the window, expecting to see life as normal; and, instead, seeing things the same as when they left to go to the *MegaBodega*.

It was almost time to think about dinner before they recuperated from their expedition to the store for supplies.

Chapter 7

David wiped his mouth with the napkin and settled back in his chair. Smiling at Alicia, he proclaimed, "Well, that sure was good. I always have liked chocolate cake, especially when it is plastered with chocolate fudge icing. Actually, the cake is merely…"

"I know, I know…a vehicle for the icing." Alicia, who had heard it dozens, hundreds, maybe thousands of times before, finished his sentence with him. Both broke out laughing, holding their sides as their amusement became almost hysterical. It took a good five minutes for them to get themselves under control. It was not all that funny, but the laugh was good for both of them—it broke the tension and deep foreboding feelings that they had harbored for a day and a half. The moment had healing effect on each of them.

Collapsed back into their chairs, they each took deep breaths and looked at each other across the flickering candle and remains of their meal. David sensed Alicia's relief but also her weariness and worry. Neither had adjusted to the new situation, but that would take a while. They were no strangers to the process of grieving and had barely started on that journey of so many unknowns. It took so long to run the gamut of feelings and with such sudden change it might take months to process it. Or maybe years.

They had shared many good and some bad moments in their life. Especially difficult was the year that David spent advising the CIA in the Middle East. He was gone for several months at a stretch, leaving Alicia to cope with the kids in an obscure Asian backwater country. Added to that was his inability because of the top secret operation and clearance, until now, to tell her where he had been working or what he was doing. Only recently he had been able to give her more details about his time away and why it had such an impact on his life. The silence for so many years had been very difficult for both of them, especially given the fact that they had a very close marriage and kept no secrets from each other.

On the other hand, there had been many beautiful moments; quiet walks in the evening up and down the Champs-Elysees in Paris, the Paseo de la Reforma in Mexico City, Fifth Avenue in New York City and around Tiananmen Square in the heart of Beijing; exotic vacations in Tahiti, diving along the Great Barrier Reef in Australia, climbing to the top of Maccu Pichu in Peru, exploring the back streets of Hong Kong; exquisite dinners atop the Space Needle in Seattle, along the Seine River in Paris and at that jungle lodge deep in the Ecuadorian rain forest. Then there were simple pleasures such as playing with the kids at a neighborhood playground a block from their apartment in Prague, a lazy New Year's Day transiting the Panama Canal on the bridge of a tramp steamer or bringing home fresh shrimp and rich papayas from a local market just blocks from the ocean in pre-civil war Monrovia.

And, they had faced challenges: raising two precocious, third-culture children, adapting to life in a dozen or more different settings in far-flung places around the globe, and the latest; adjusting to the empty nest and trying to decide where to retire when your children and grandchildren are nomadic and not likely to settle anywhere for quite some while.

As they remained quiet for a while, letting what might be their last "normal" meal settle, the enormity of their situation seemed to come to both of them simultaneously.

"You know, Hon," David began. "We have gathered all of this food and water for several months as if we were setting out on some expedition from which we will return in three or four weeks. It's almost like we expect everything to return to normal when we get back so we don't have to think much beyond the immediate future."

"You're right. I was thinking about what happens after the fridge completely warms up and the veggies and fruit at the MegaBodega rots away and the mice eat up all the crackers and the flour all turns buggy and there is no more water in the roof tank and the car doesn't run anymore and we run out of toilet paper!"

They both laughed again, but it didn't explode or linger like it did before.

"Yeah, and what happens when the roving dogs multiply and join into rabid packs and we run out of operable gas tanks to run the stove and we don't have any more ice and we develop some new physical malady that we can neither diagnose nor certainly treat and the volcano decides to erupt and bury us in ash and…"

"Stop!" Alicia exclaimed. "That's enough. Some of those we can deal with while others are so far out and so far down the road, hopefully, that we can't possibly deal with them now. What we need to concentrate on is gathering resources and planning on survival for the intermediate future. Let's try to get off this negative thinking streak."

"Survival," David mused. "You're right, as long as we don't get voted off of the island," he joked, referring to a line from a popular TV program of the same name.

David stayed up long after Alicia crawled into bed totally spent by exhaustion after such an active and emotionally draining day. He had his legal pad open to a new sheet and was busy scribbling by candlelight.

<u>Issues to solve</u>

<u>Food-</u>
Garden needs- seeds, tools, space (vacant lots)
Veggies, grains
Local fruit trees, bushes in neighborhood- bananas, oranges, papayas, mangoes
Meat/protein-hunting-wild animals we could eat: birds, monkeys, armadillo, squirrels

Animals we can find on other's property:
Cows, goats, pigs, chickens/eggs
Stock of food from stores-canned goods
Staples: flour, rice, dried beans
Preserving the food-solar panels to run a refrigerator and freezer
Guns and ammo, bows and arrows

He paused for a moment as he realized the enormity of the job ahead and the speed with which some things would need to be done to keep foods edible. But he sighed and went back to his list. No point dwelling on it too long.

<u>Storage issues-</u>
Barrels to catch rain from the roof
Containers to get water from the nearby river, canning jars

Then he put a little star next to this item indicating the importance of it for survival. He wrote: Bottled water for the short-term use.

<u>Energy needs-</u>
Generator(s)
Solar

He thought to himself, "This is easy. I have seen enough hoses wound in a ring on the roof of houses collecting solar heat. I know how to get plenty of hot water. But electricity for lights was another issue." He knew he would have to figure that out. Then he added more items to his list.

    Windmills
    Batteries

    <u>Security-</u>
    Stay in apartment—protected for now—harder for animals to reach
    Stray animals, dogs,
    Hostile people (if there are <u>any</u> people)
    Build a fence/wall around the empty lots for gardening if they are not already walled
    Wild fires that might sweep across the valley

    <u>Other</u>
    What to do with decomposing bodies
    Gas for vehicles

    <u>Tools and building materials</u>

    David sighed again and quit writing. There were so many other issues that needed to be tackled such as transportation, health care, repairs, innovations with plumbing no longer working as normal with no electricity and the list went on in his mind. But, he was too tired to take his list any further. "So much to think about", he muttered under his breath.
    Besides, he was struggling again with the issue of whether they were truly alone in the battle for survival or whether, somewhere, there were others,

compiling their own lists, setting up their own protective barriers though looking for companionship, help, and assistance as they, too, struggled to survive. Often he found his spirits lifted as he considered that in this city of a million souls, if they were still alive, there must be others.

Yet, in the course of two full days, they had not seen, heard nor sensed any indication that anyone else—benevolent or malevolent—was around to share with them the enormity of the task.

He looked over the list again. "My high school English teachers would have flunked me for this disorganized list," he thought as he smiled to himself. But, it served his purpose and allowed him to fall asleep as soon as his head touched the pillow.

Chapter 8

"The cats!" Alicia seemed to startle herself along with David as she jumped out of her chair. Then, realizing that she was still eating breakfast, she slumped back down, but quickly shoveled in the last of her cereal and fruit.

"What are you talking about," asked David, recovering slightly from the sudden outburst.

"Pablo and Maria's cats. I totally forgot about them. The poor things! I need to go over there right away and make sure they are ok."

Pablo and Maria Von Boem were their closest friends in Costa Brava. They lived about a fifteen minute walk away and so David and Alicia had agreed to take care of their cats while they were attending an academic conference in Germany.

Like David and Alicia, the Von Boem's had lived most of their adult lives overseas. However, unlike David and Alicia who suffered from wanderlust and thus had lived in the four corners of the earth, Pablo and Maria had lived in Costa Brava ever since they completed their doctoral work in Heidelberg, Germany and accepted a teaching position at the National University in San Juan. Both had degrees in world literature and taught the classics to students from throughout Central America. In fact, they had spent so much time in the Spanish-speaking world that they had long ago adopted the Spanish equivalents of their English names, Paul and Mary, so that in recent years even English-speaking people called them Pablo and Maria. Only their last name gave away their German heritage.

David had met Pablo at a conference over a decade ago in London and their friendship, along with that of their wives, had grown over the years. Together they sailed the Rhine River in Germany and cruised down the Yangtze River in China before it was flooded. On several occasions, they skied at the fantastic mountain resorts surrounding Bariloche in Argentina.

In fact, it was their friendship that drew David and Alicia to accept the teaching positions offered to them (with Pablo's help) at the National University in Costa Brava several years prior. And, it was one of the reasons that they were thinking of settling down permanently in this country which often had been called a paradise by many.

"I'll go with you," David said. He didn't want Alicia going into an empty house, or more importantly, walking along the empty streets of their neighborhood.

So far neither of them had detected any sign of life anywhere in the city. The last couple of nights they still, from their second floor balcony, stood scanning with David's binoculars to see if they could catch the slightest hint of light flickering even from a candle lit in someone's house or the sweep of a flashlight from another human being also craving human companionship Just like the first night when

David waited for lights to appear on the mountains, there were none.

During the day David did a similar scan of the visible streets, still hoping to catch some kind, any kind, of human activity. But so far they had sensed nothing. So why should he worry that Alicia walk by herself to check on the cats? He could not explain his uneasy feeling about it.

Perhaps his sense of concern was that there was so much evidence that at one time the city had housed over a million people. Houses spread out along random streets that ran up and down hillsides. Gleaming high-rise apartment buildings that had been built to ring the huge Carolina Park still stood out against the sky, reflecting a beautiful image from their glass panes each evening as the sun went down.

And, as more proof that there were once people around the city, every day David and Alicia witnessed explosions from various sectors of the city, spewing smoke and steam and who knows what kind of chemicals into the air. David always shuddered as he realized that the explosions signaled that people were no longer controlling various manufacturing and storage facilities that were erupting because they required human intervention to remain under control.

One such explosion not too far from their apartment had sent a particularly acrid smell throughout their neighborhood. Alicia ran to close the windows against the burning fumes that continued to seep into their apartment through the various cracks despite her valiant attempts to shut it out.

"That smell is horrible," David had said. I can't even guess what it might be, and maybe I don't want to know. You have more of a science background than I do, Hon."

Not wanting to breathe deep enough to answer until she had sealed up the house the best she could. At the time, she then began to think what it might be. "It smells a bit like an acid. Those fumes could sting like crazy and burn our eyes. That is one reason why chemistry teachers use a hood to blow the fumes out…to say nothing of what it could do to our lungs."

His response was a concerned, "It doesn't sound good at all."

"Something that strong likely isn't," Alicia responded with a concern in her voice that David immediately picked up on. "Hopefully, not much seeped in, and I hope that with this breeze it blows off," he reflected. *"How much more can go wrong?"* she thought to herself.

Obviously she must have said it out loud, perhaps in a soft voice that David could hear, because he had responded with an equally soft voice. "I don't know.

On the one hand, it seemed perfectly safe for either of them to go anywhere they wanted. There appeared to be no threat from people of mal-intent. In fact there appeared to be no people around at all. But then, they were only into the third day of this whole new world, and neither of them had any idea what might be lurking around the corner, in another neighborhood, in a nearby house or even in the sky overhead.

David walked with Alicia to the Von Boem's house about six blocks away. He felt better to go rather than let her walk by herself. The route took them in a different direction than they had traveled the past two days. They worked their way through their quiet (now too quiet) neighborhood of well-kept houses, across the boulevard lined with trees budding with beautiful pink flowers late in this rainy season, across the two-square block neighborhood park where they often went to read or just watch the kids play and on to their friend's house.

The walk was still pretty, though marred by more dead bodies, stray dogs looking a little threatening and the lack of the usual chaos of crazy drivers, horns, smoking buses David and Alicia had learned to almost love. The silence that was almost deafening, despite birds chirping in the trees, was still eerie.

Pablo and Maria had raised three children in Costa Brava and as a result of having lived in one place for over thirty years had accumulated a large collection of books and musical albums as well as walls covered with art work from their travels. Plus, they had the usual conglomeration of stuff that homeowners have anywhere when they haven't moved for several years.

David smiled to himself as he remembered what Alicia always said absolutely every time they had moved. "The best way to clean a house and get rid of what you don't need is to move—especially overseas." That was absolutely true. International relocation is expensive either for the employer or for the employed, whoever is paying for the move. And, with the recent trend toward shipping everything by air, international vagabonds like David and Alicia needed to lighten the load as much as possible with every move.

So, when they arrived in San Juan, they did not bring much with them to represent their 40 years of marriage. They always bought new furniture in each location, as well as appliances, bed linens and other common items. What they carried with them was David's extensive collection of books and their museum-quality souvenirs from the countries in which they had lived. But this time they hadn't brought too much clothing. They were moving from a post in an area where the weather was cold to Costa Brava's tropical climate and figured that other than a few sweaters and jackets and one winter coat each to take with them when they traveled north, it just wasn't worth transporting all of that heavy clothing. Besides, the department stores in the downtown were well stocked with quality clothing more fitting to the climate.

Pablo and Maria, in contrast, had decided to purchase a single-family house with a substantial yard, rather than pour money into a rented apartment.

Also, both were avid gardeners. Maria, particularly, prided herself in her rich tropical flower garden that ringed both the small front yard and the expansive back yard that was surrounded by a 15-foot wall topped with barbed wire. Inside that almost prison-like perimeter she had planted bountiful tropical flowers, fruit trees and lush palms that gave the entire yard the atmosphere of a tropical paradise.

When they got together, Maria would recount the birds they had seen in their back yard, attracted to the wonderful colorful vegetation and blossoms: great Kiskadee thrushes, blue-gray tanagers, and grackles. She happily spouted off the Latin names: Pitangus sulphuratus, Turdus grayi and all the others. Though it did not interest Alicia to know the names of the birds, it was obvious that Maria took great pride in knowing and keeping track of them.

Pablo, meanwhile, constantly worked at his manicured grass and the exotic orchids that hung along all of the back yard walls and from tree branches arching over the property.

Over the years, the two couples had passed many pleasant evenings in this yard grilling tender steaks and discussing the peculiarities of various faculty members they knew both at the National University and in professional societies around the world.

Now, as they approached their friend's house and its idyllic setting, David and Alicia grew silent. They thought not only of their friends, but also their own children in Florida and El Salvador. Both of them seemed to realize simultaneously that they had no idea whether anyone they knew or had ever known, close to them or distant, was alive or dead or if they would ever see them again. It seemed unlikely, judging from what they had experienced in the last days.

Alicia wiped a tear with her sleeve as David opened the Von Boem's door and listened. Not that he expected to hear anything—after all, their friends were out of the country. But, with the extraordinary events of the past few days, they didn't know what to expect.

They were greeted by two very hungry and hyper cats demanding to know why they hadn't been fed and why they had been left alone for such a long time without care or comfort.

"If only you knew," David mused to himself. "If only you knew," he repeated.

The couple bustled around the house, opening a few windows to let in some fresh air, feeding the cats which whimpered and danced around with impatience as they got the food out, then gulped it down as if they hadn't eaten in days—which, come to think of it, they hadn't.

After a few walk-throughs of the house and around the pristine tropical garden outside, along with the gathering of some bananas, papayas and coconuts from the various plants, they locked up and started back home, taking the Von Boems' cats with them in a cage they found in a *bodega*.

"You have to ask why you did that," Alicia said after David locked the door.

"Did what?"

"Locked the door. With no one else around, who is going to take anything?" The couple both knew the answer. Some habits die hard, and locking doors is one you first learn living overseas in some countries.

The couple walked home deep in their own thoughts much of the way.

Finally, David broke the silence, "What are we going to do with two more cats? And what are we going to feed them?"

Alicia didn't have much of an answer, but added as if off in space, "I don't know. But we could not leave them there to starve to death. My question is how well will they get along with our cat."

"I guess we will see, won't we? And, we will have to figure out the food issue."

"Did we get all the cat food Pablo and Maria had, or do I need to go back and then also go to the *MaxiBodega* for what I can find there?"

Alicia hesitantly added, "Maybe they will have to get used to the mixture I made up for our black cat we had when we lived in Ecuador. She took to it pretty well when she got hungry enough. Let's just get them home and solve the problems as they came along. It seems that these cats are not the biggest challenges we have to solve, right?"

"Yes, that's for sure. One thing at a time." David conceded.

"We might as well have a little levity about our problems. Let's remember the saying, 'How do you eat an elephant?' Sometimes this whole thing seems like an elephant."

"You eat it one bite at a time." And they both chuckled a bit, releasing a little tension that had built up with each challenge. And they fell silent again.

Chapter 9

As they approached their apartment they broke the spell and began to chatter about the myriad of things they were noticing: the change in the air—from pollution to a freshness common only after a tropical downpour; yet in contrast, the occasional whiff of a decomposing human body or animal, and of course that horrible stinging smell after the explosion. They noted blowing newspapers littering the streets as well as whimpering, sulking, occasionally barking or snarling dogs as they walked by fenced-in yards. And, there were always other former pets running through the neighborhood dragging broken leashes or ropes, if they were lucky enough to break their restraint.

Back at home, David pulled out his legal pad and began to peruse his list from the night before.

"You know Hon, I'm not sure where to start," he said.

"I know what you mean. But, surely we have things that we ought to be doing." Alicia responded.

"Oh, that's not the problem, believe me," David said. "The problem is that we have so many things that we need to do that it's hard to know where to start; what our priorities should be."

"Well, we brought enough food over here yesterday to keep us going for several months," Alicia observed. "So, we probably don't need to go back to the store for anything right now."

"Right," David agreed. "But that's not where my confusion comes from. We *are* in pretty good shape in many ways. However, we need to be thinking long term and planning for things we don't even know about yet."

"Like what?"

"Well, assuming that the lights aren't going to go back on and the trucks bringing supplies in aren't going to resume their work and the water is going to eventually be used up or drain out of the water tanks and reservoirs, and we are either going to run out of gas, or the car is going to break down, or the gasoline that we have is going to go bad, which it will eventually. As hard as it is emotionally we need to be thinking creatively about preparing for the future while we do everything with what we have right now."

"So, again, like what?"

Well, first, we need to assume that we won't have motorized transportation forever, unless I turn into a genius and come up with some alternative form of fuel. So, we need to enter into a gathering stage where we can bring here, or close to here, anything that we might need in the next few years that would be useful or necessary for us and that we couldn't transport well without a car or truck."

"A truck? Where are you going to get that?" Alicia questioned. "We have a trooper, but that's a far cry from a truck."

"Hon, calm down and think for a minute. Remember yesterday when I said that I never thought I would be a looter?"

She thought for a minute. "Well, yes."

"So, yesterday I became a professional looter, and so did you!"

He grinned at her wickedly at the thought of becoming common thieves and driving away with several carloads of goods as they did the day before.

She returned his grin. "OK, so you are telling me that now you are going to become a car thief? Or, even a truck thief?"

"That's the idea. There are hundreds or thousands of trucks around this city, many of them full of gas or diesel, just waiting to be of service to us. All we have to do is to stop by, extract the keys from their non-resistant owners, and drive off with a new Ford or Chevy or International Harvester pickup."

Alicia mumbled. "My husband—a common thief!"

"Oh, no," David challenged her. "Not just a common thief. A specialized, very intentional, professional thief who will merely appropriate a ve-*hi*-cle (he said it policeman style) for a period of time to complete a job. We can even return it to its owner when we are done. If we want to," he added after a moment of silence.

Alicia sighed, "Sometimes this thing is just too much," she complained. "I know that what you are suggesting is what we need to do, but it's so different, so contrary to our values, and the way we have lived, and how we brought up our children…"

Her sentence drifted off and she started to cry. Lightly at first, but then in huge sobs that shook her body. David quickly moved toward her, taking her in his arms. He let her cry for a while, and then, when she stopped shaking and the crying diminished, he said, "Hon, I know it's hard and there will be times that we need to cry. But right now it is time that we get our act together and start thinking methodically about what we are going to need in the very long run and where we are going to get it. And, we need to get as much of it while we still have operating vehicles and fuel."

Alicia wiped her eyes and looked at him. "I know you are right. Just, please, have patience with me as I try to work it through and do all of what I need to do as well. It is just all such a change all at once." And then added, "It is all so draining, emotionally exhausting."

A simple "yes" was his response before charging ahead with their plans.

"OK, let's do some quick thinking," David said as soon as she seemed ready to talk. "First, although we have enough packaged and canned food to last a while, if this thing goes on, and I'm beginning to think that it will, we will soon have to think about gathering and growing our own food. We are going to become like early people who were hunters and gathers as well as subsistence farmers in order to keep alive."

"At least we don't have to make our own tools, thank goodness!" she blurted out.

"We are going to have figure out where we will gather food, where we will plant crops and what tools we will need to do that kind of work. And, doing that is going to involve a giant personal emotional change, from class-room work to farmers, mechanics and manual laborers."

"Not only that, but we need to adapt to a style of thinking and acting that is so contrary to what we lived before," he reflected. "It is one thing when we grow a small garden for fun, and when we have to grow to live, to stay alive."

"What do you mean?" she asked.

"Well, we are now living in a situation where traditional ethical guidelines that were operable in normal civilization need to be reconsidered. Before, we had a system of behavior but now we are living in a totally changed world where we are practicing what is known as situation ethics, where values have to be weighed with survival, and some of our previous assumptions need to be, perhaps, adjusted."

Alicia was silent for a few moments. Then, having recovered from her sudden burst of grief, agreed that it was time to get to work and move ahead. They knew that time was precious in this new lifestyle, and it could not be wasted.

Chapter 10

They took a quick spin around the neighborhood before heading out to the huge *Super Ferretería* hardware store that had opened not too far from their apartment. It had been such a wonderful addition in Costa Brava, being able to get just about anything they wanted, from paint to nails and everything in between. David found it to be fun to explore the giant business on his day off, often going by himself since it was not such an interesting activity for her. But then he reserved the fabric and sewing goods for Alicia's excursions by herself. Those individual trips had given them a nice day to themselves and a little space. Most of the time they were together, but time alone was good too.

As they cruised the area around their neighborhood, they took note of various mangos, avocado, guava and other fruit trees poking their tops above the barbed wire-lined walls. From place to place they found banana bushes pushing up from spacious manicured gardens. And, within five blocks of the house, they found a half-dozen empty lots that David figured with a lot work could be turned into ample gardens in the rich, tropical soil.

"One of the few advantages of the walled security even in some vacant lots is that it will keep the marauding dogs and other animals, also looking for food, out of the garden once we get the plants growing," he said. "All I have to do is figure how to break down the gates without damaging them so much that I can't close them again."

Alicia grunted in agreement. It seemed like an awful lot of physical work that neither of them were used to. "How are you going to get into locked buildings and yards, and then how are you going to plow up the acreage that we will need?" she wondered.

"No sweat," said David in a forced, cocky manner. "First, I plan to pick up a crowbar or two and other tools at the *Super Ferretería*, then I figure on breaking in to that locksmith place near the mall and seeing if I can find some master keys that will just allow me to walk into any place I please."

"Oh, right, and when that fails?" Alicia was beginning to doubt her husband's fanciful dreams.

"Well, first of all, have a little confidence and faith in me," he said with a little smile. "Second, I have a few other ideas. Remember the day that we were at the Baker's house on the other side of town—the day that they were almost broken in to?"

"Yeeessss….," Alicia hesitated. "What does that have to do with anything?"

"Well, the thief had almost broken through the bars and gotten access to the window glass by using an old tire jack to spread the bars apart. It was crude, but it was working…until he got caught and ran away."

"Well, I suppose that might work, but what if it doesn't?

"Simple," David replied. "Just last week I saw on television where the cops were trying to break into a drug runner's safe-house somewhere in the city. When they couldn't get through the gate, they just connected a chain to a pickup truck and, with tires squealing, jerked the gate off of its hinges. So much for high-tech security."

Alicia slid down in her seat and looked pensively out of the windows. Within a few minutes they arrived in the large parking lot of the huge superstore which had revolutionized the supply of building and hardware supplies in the capital city.

Until its opening six months earlier, customers had to hunt out little hole-in-the wall stores in a four square block of downtown to see which one had just what they wanted. There was no such concept as one-stop shopping. Instead, a shopper had to go door-to-door to seek which store had drill bits, which had nuts and bolts, which carried barbed wire and where one might find plumbing or electrical supplies. The search for a single tiny part could take the better part of a morning. The one nice thing was that all small hardware stores were grouped in a single block while other outlets such as clothing or craft stores were grouped in other neighboring locations, making shopping a lot easier. The problem, of course, was that if Alicia wanted lace or ribbon and material, those things might be separated by several blocks. But the system worked, and it was kind of nice.

Goods were available, just spread out. Almost anything that a person would want could be found somewhere in the city. The challenge was to figure out where the section in town was. People who had lived in San Juan knew and would help.

But, with the opening of the new Argentinean-run super hardware and building supply store, most items, as least those that were fairly common, could be found in one building, something like those huge hardware depots in the United States.

Alicia was still going to the material and sewing needs part of San Juan while David could now easily go to the large hardware store.

David steered their sturdy Trooper into the basically empty parking lot. There was none of the hustle and bustle that marked most days as construction crews and contractors came and went with the supplies for their day's work. Since the incident had happened at night, the few cars were likely those of the night watchman and the stockers who worked those late hours so they had free movement of equipment without endangering customers.

Alicia shuddered as she thought of those people lying dead and decaying on the floor. "David, this is not going to be a very pleasant experience with the smell and bodies."

"Yes. Not a pleasant thought. I think I will open a doors on opposite sides of the store to get a cross breeze and carry the smell out."

"That will help a bit. Will I ever get used to it? It makes every trip to a new place a traumatic experience, doesn't it?"

"Yeah," David agreed, "But we have to push ahead."

The main entrance doors were closed and appeared to all be chained shut. David hated the idea of having to shatter the huge plate glass windows and break the chains, so he made his way around to the back of the store where trucks pulled up to unload their deliveries. There, the huge loading dock was wide open and the pair entered the building.

David made his way through to the front, holding his breath as much as possible against the stench. He hoped there was a way to open up to get a cross breeze, and happily found a door that was easy to open with a flick of a lock. That was a relief.

He would close up as he left, not that anyone else would be coming in, but to keep out animals looking for dog food or rats looking for edible grains.

It was a fairly new store, and well stocked for such a business. But it was dark with the power outage. The first task was to find some battery powered lights to see into the corners of the building that had no natural light from the doors or skylights.

When it first opened, the pent-up demand for certain items quickly cleaned out some areas of the store, but the managers had rapidly restocked and now almost everything was available.

"Oh, Hon, here is the shopping list. Let's bring what we need here to the loading dock and then we can shuttle things we buy…uh…take…back home."

"That's a good idea," Alicia affirmed. "But some of the things you want are pretty heavy—like a rototiller, and a large water tank or two. How are we going to handle that?"

David had known that the larger, heavy items might present a challenge. Then, he spied a good-sized delivery truck at the end of the loading dock. Also, there were forklifts that the stockers had been using. He hoped both would solve their problem.

Quickly, he took off to see if the truck was operable, had any gasoline, and whether the keys to operate it were anywhere nearby. It appeared to be in good shape, but no keys were to be found in the ignition nor was there any sign of the driver near the dock.

"We'll look around the store and see if we find the body of anyone who looks like a driver who might have keys," he said when he returned to where Alicia was standing. "I just hope that the driver didn't park it there and go home. But, maybe we can locate another large vehicle somewhere that would be helpful."

Finding a new truck was not an issue. The driver had stood talking to an employee as the stockers unloaded his truck. He lay not far from the door with the shipping papers and keys in his hand. A few minutes later he would have been on his way with his empty truck. The couple felt so lucky and grateful.

Flashlights in hand that they had picked up at the *MegaBodega* where they got the food, and with a little help from a scattering of skylights, the couple spent the next two hours hauling goods to the loading dock. They found items they had not even thought about when they were making their lists. They added them to the growing piles waiting to be loaded. Gardening tools, bags of fertilizer and insecticide, crowbars, ladders, a rototiller, several dozen gas tanks to fuel their cooking stove, and a number of large storage cabinets were placed in the pile of things to move to the apartment. Much to Alicia's disgust, David had several rifles and a few shotguns and ammunition that he procured by smashing the cases in which they were displayed.

"I guess I'm going to have to learn how to shoot these things," David grinned. "The Agency gave me a quick training course, but I have always been scared of them so I never even thought about using them."

"I wish you didn't need to have them around the house," Alicia sighed. "But, I understand that they may be necessary—especially when you are away working on a garden plot, and if or when we decide to go hunting for some meat."

"I agree," David admitted. "I don't like them either. And, wouldn't it be ironic if, with evidently no people around, I had to shoot the first person we ran across?" Both were silent as they loaded the smaller items into the Trooper and the larger items into the truck and began the drive home.

Weaving around abandoned vehicles while avoiding the already-existing, numerous pot-holes provided a challenge. They passed cars in the median, off the road, and some blocking the lanes as they made their way home.

But, nowhere, on the trip to or back from the *Super Ferretería* did they still see any evidence of one living human being.

Chapter 11

At first, the daily routine was difficult on both of them. But with some of the worst problems solved and a little time to deal with the emotional toll, things seemed to be a little easier. Their activities seemed to become more routine to them both. Still not exactly fun, but manageable.

David and Alicia had tried to keep themselves in as good a shape as modern, comfortable urban living permitted. They had joined a gym and worked out regularly on the treadmill and bicycles. They did a little muscle building exercise, but neither had really enjoyed it. They did it because they wanted to stay healthy as they aged, or perhaps, more accurately, they felt they had to.

One thing they both loved was hiking. In fact, hiking and camping had been what brought them together in the beginning, and they had continued to be outdoors as much as possible during their child-rearing and working years.

In Costa Brava they occasionally went with a local hiking club up into the mountains where they climbed to elevations of several thousand feet and then dropped down into the valleys where clear rushing mountain rivers cut deep gorges through the pristine jungle, with its myriad of animals, flowers and plants...as well as plenty of snakes.

But, that kind of exercise, while good for keeping them in shape, was far different from a daily life now made more challenging by the lack of power in the home for electrically operated tools and the necessity to provide for their own needs.

Within a day or two after gathering the hardware and gardening equipment, David set out to begin preparing some of the neighboring lots for gardening. He found the weight of the rototiller to be almost impossible for him to lift in and out of the Trooper, so soon found one of those "car creeper" type wagons that mechanics use to work under an automobile. Using it as a means of transport, he moved from yard to yard, and within a week had nearly two acres of land plowed up. But, from there his work was by hand.

Using a shovel, hoe and rake, he removed rocks, tore out tall weeds, carried away debris dumped there by someone who had no trash pickup. With the clearing, went the rats and other critters who lived among the garbage. David then prepared the tropical soil for planting by adding fertilizer and other nutrients he had found in the gardening section of the hardware store.

As a result, he came home exhausted every night. His muscles ached, and he barely made it up the stairs.

Life was not any easier for Alicia. It was up to her to maintain the house and to somehow organize all of the goods that they had brought home from various stores around the community. Very quickly she learned that the house could not possibly store everything that they had gathered.

David began to fill up exterior empty spaces with boxes of supplies and other items that they had appropriated. They quickly filled the four parking spots and patios normally used by the other tenants. He designated some for food, others for cleaning and maintenance supplies and still others for gardening equipment. He also gained access to neighboring yards and homes.

In each place, to avoid any potential water damage from tropical downpour run-off, they were careful to place items off the floor on wooden 2x4s or pallets that they scrounged in various warehouses. And, in each location, David broke into the facility very carefully to assure that he could lock the doors or gates behind him. Some, he had even been able to open with one of two master keys that he took from a locksmith store that he had broken into, with some surprise. "You would think that a locksmith place would be one of the most difficult places to burglarize," he had told Alicia after gaining access in only five minutes. "Some people just think that they are invincible I guess."

Preparing for growing, hunting and harvesting food was the most difficult thing that the couple faced, being urban dwellers whose food was delivered to vast shopping complexes or large markets by truck. David and Alicia had very little recent experience in food gathering other than by driving to the mall. In his early years David had planted a simple garden, but even growing tomatoes successfully had been a challenge for him. Now, they began to realize what it took when life was normal to get their food grown, harvested and to the market for them to buy it. Both gained a new respect for the whole process.

David learned that he must be systematic and thorough if he was to raise crops that would not only fill their stomachs but also provide them with a nourishing and balanced diet.

Wisely, he decided to pace his work and not wear himself out or injure his back or limbs. He always felt himself fortunate to have avoided any major bone or muscular injuries and decided that he wanted to keep his record intact.

The sun shone most of the day until the late afternoon storms arrived and David soon found that his biggest complaints were thirst and sunburn problems. With the sun rising at around 5 a.m. and the early morning being the coolest part of the day, he quickly adapted to the ways of standard time preferred by farmers who rose early, worked early, took a rest or *siesta* and retired early for the day. Not wanting to overdo, he often found himself returning home by two in the afternoon, hungry and tired, and calling it a day.

"You know Hon, maybe I would have made a good farmer after all, not having given it a thought until it was a matter of life and death," David exclaimed one day after a rather satisfying stint at breaking dirt and raking it out into a smooth field. "But, I have to admit that even with my precautions of not wearing myself out, I'm pretty sore and tired."

Alicia agreed that he needed to pace his schedule and so she tried to have a hearty meal in place when he returned for *siesta*. Drawing on the large store of packaged and canned food, she was usually able to put a balanced meal in front of him.

Protein, especially meat, was another issue, though she knew there were plenty of vegetarians in the world. They just weren't two of them…at least not yet. Alicia had cooked or dried some of the meat that they found in the various supermarkets, but the lack of refrigerator or freezer limited what she could keep. She was aware that meat could be canned, but did not have a pressure cooker to seal it so it would not spoil. Nor did she know much about it. *"Who cans food these days?"* she thought to herself.

Finally, one day the two decided that not only would they have to develop a farming lifestyle but would also have to learn hunting skills if they were to have meat and survive. They would wait to see if they would have to become vegetarian.

The hunt for protein from animals was less successful. Initially, David and Alicia were aware of a few chickens and a rooster which are always present even in the most upscale neighborhoods in developing countries. Though David had threatened to kill the noisy, neighboring roosters which began their wake-up call around 2 a.m., he decided that eggs and chicken on his plate were more desirable, and he could learn to sleep through the noise.

To help with the sound problem, the couple installed the brood in an enclosed yard about three blocks away, hoping that roving wild animals wouldn't get the eggs and chickens before they did. They could make a daily trip there to feed the birds and harvest what was edible.

Alicia's first question was, "How do you pluck it? You are going to take care of that, right?", she said looking hopefully at David. As they were whizzing by a country *finca* years ago in their car, she had seen a woman swing a chicken over her head, and then whap it against her porch rail. And, she had seen her father hang a chicken by its feet from her favorite climbing tree in their backyard and then cut off its head. She was having nothing to do with that part of it. Cook it? Yes. That she could handle.

David agreed to his side of the bargain. He would kill away from their apartment where she would see or hear nothing from the poor critter.

All this, once again, reminded them of how much they were city people. Like all else the last few days until this....what would you call it? Disaster? Event? Tragedy? Incident?...there would be a learning curve if they wanted to survive, which they did.

Suddenly switching the subject without totally solving the chicken problem, at least in Alicia's mind, David blurted out, "A blowgun!"

"A what?" Alicia asked. "What are you talking about now?"

"A blowgun, Hon," David responded. "Do you remember those long blowguns that we saw along the Amazon in Peru?" David recalled the time he saw a pilot loading a tourist's souvenir blowgun onto a single engine Cessna. It went from the very tail to the cockpit of the plane. "That's exactly what we need to hunt down some meat."

"Well, I suppose so," Alicia mused. "But, what about the gun and rifle you got? Wouldn't that be a little more efficient and modern?"

"Maybe so," David responded, "But you know I've never been an *aficionado* of guns, and, besides, they scare me. I'm afraid that I might shoot myself in the foot or the leg." Adding, "And I am not familiar enough with hunting with a gun to figure how long ammunition will last."

"Yeah, but you also could shoot your own foot with a blowgun if you aren't careful," Alicia replied with a mischievous grin.

"Well, yes, perhaps, but at least the treatment wouldn't involve cutting into myself and having to perform surgery on my own leg." David said, shuddering at the thought.

"I suppose so, but what are you going to put on your darts to poison the poor animals when you do shoot them? Have you thought about that?"

David thought for a few minutes. "I'm not sure," he said. "But, when I was by the mission hospital the other day I spent an hour or so rummaging through some medicine closets. Surely I could find something there that I could put on the end of the dart to stun the animal."

"Sure," Alicia said with a hint of sarcasm in her voice. "Just let me know when you are ready for your first hunt so I can alert 911!"

"You know David, this is a ridiculous conversation. Let's raise chickens and see if there are other edible animals grazing in fields on the outskirts of San Juan we can bring in closer. I have seen goats not so far from here. I'd say, let's wait a bit to worry about this issue of hunting. Yes?"

"Yes, let's," he replied.

David was more certain about his farming enterprise then hunting. On their drive around the neighborhood on their first scavenging expedition, they had found several yards with prolific fruit trees bearing everything from mangos to papayas, bananas to oranges and limes. And later while in one yard he had even discovered a favorite, rhubarb. A while later in another he was so excited to find a large patch of blackberries. Maybe with a little sugar, Alicia would make some of her most wonderful blackberry jam.

The problem with collecting the produce from the trees was keeping the yards around them passable through new growth of grass and weeds. Actually, with each problem they solved another was right around the corner related to the first. It seemed endless at times.

They seemed to jump from subject to subject as they continued to think through their needs and desires. If they were going to make a go of all this, it would take constant thought, planning and self-learning. Many times they never finished one subject, like the chickens and how to handle that, before moving to the next topic or issue at hand. Eventually, they would get back to unfinished business and solve many of the problems.

One of those issues was how to sustain food for a long time, perhaps for years. Downtown, around the old central market, they discovered a seed store that provided all kinds of resources for the various truck gardeners who worked the steep slopes of the Izkatzu Volcano that towered over the east side of the city. Canisters of various vegetable seeds lined the walls and they even found some potato sprouts that were waiting for a farmer to pick up.

David and Alicia brought home most of the seed that they found and carefully packaged much of it in air-tight bags to extend its shelf life. He hoped to be able to get and dry his own seeds from the produce, but until that point he had lots on hand.

Measuring out what he thought he could manage the first year, he divided his gardening into the different lots that he had prepared around the neighborhood. He decided to plant duplicate plots in at least two different gardens in case some damage or disaster in one lot destroyed that crop. In the first months, he would plant seeds and potato seedlings in the eight lots, giving him four different gardens duplicated in other lots.

Reading a gardening book that he picked up at the lending library at one of the private English-language schools, he carefully spaced his plants according to the instructions, and planted them close to other plants that were said to be compatible, all the time wondering if he should be certain to take the book back so as not to face an overdue fine! He chuckled as that thought passed his mind—a product of being raised in a home where his mother was a librarian. He also worked to secure each lot with fencing or wooden walls to keep out marauding animals.

Reading had always been a part of their lives, but with so much to do, it would have to be confined to learning how to stay alive, at least until they had the routine down pat.

David had discovered the raised bed method of gardening in another location when the family lived just above the large commercial operation run by immigrants from Hong Kong. Their long, four-foot wide beds raised a foot or so above the surrounding soil allowed the heavy tropical rains to soak the gardens while draining off quickly from the raised hills so as not to rot the plants or their roots. He learned a lot from watching the men work from dawn to dark on their garden. Maybe there was a reason he spent so much time watching them as he relaxed on his back porch on cooler evenings.

'The incident' as David and Alicia called that infamous day when the world as they knew it came to a screeching halt, occurred during Costa Brava's rainy season, so, they didn't need to worry about irrigation for the crops. Each day began with glorious sunshine which gave way to a copious downpour for an hour or so every afternoon. The result was that the eight gardens remained well-watered but also with plenty of hot, tropical sun to sustain the plants.

He had been concerned about the growing number of hungry, snarling dogs that were roaming the neighborhood in search of food. Left to forage for themselves after their owners died, those that managed to escape their fenced in yards were joining up and mating with wild mutts that had always made themselves at home on the city streets. Some of them were ferocious pit bulls and Rottweilers that people kept because of the growing crime problem in the city.

Now, free to roam, their wild instincts over domestic traits they possessed had led to frequent confrontations with him.

One afternoon while weeding one of the plots, a pack of roaming feral dogs broke through one of David's makeshift wooden fences and came running toward him through the patch. He immediately jumped up and began to yell and wave his hoe at the viciously barking mob. They tore through the garden, tearing up carefully placed plants that were just beginning to start growing.

David ran to the fence where he had other tools and a long carving knife that he had started to carry with him just in case. The dogs came closer, barking and snarling, and, to be truthful, scaring the breath out of him.

Finally, he was able to grab a long-handled rake and brought it down on one of the dogs. The mutt drew back and bared its teeth, growling and growing ever more threatening. David swung again with the rake, knocking the dog over with the force of the blow. Some of the other dogs backed off a bit.

David went after the wounded dog, but it quickly regained its footing and started to run toward him. David charged, waving the rake, and yelling with all his might. Finally frightened, the dogs ran for the breached fence, squeezed through the hole and ran off down the street.

David collapsed against the fence and breathed a sigh of relief. Not wanting to risk a repeat attack, he spent the rest of the afternoon patching the hole, moving some lumber and other objects to insure that it couldn't happen again.

Another problem plaguing David and Alicia was the various insects, especially cutter ants, with which they had become familiar with during their time in the jungles of Ecuador. The ants could strip a six-foot high decorative bush of its leaves in an eight-hour work day. These voracious bugs seemed to leave most of the vegetables alone, but liked to strip some of the larger plants. They particularly liked those which bore fruit. While not killing the plants, they set growth back for several days while the plants struggled to produce new leaves.

Even though the creatures were a problem to back-yard plants and gardens, out in the jungle David and Alicia had spent a lot of time just watching the ants carry pieces of leaves, many times their size, climb up trees and actually form noticeable paths to their nest underground. The ants would not eat the leaves, but waited until they grew mold. That is what they actually ate.

David didn't like to use insecticides, but after reading in some gardening books about natural methods, within several months he was able to produce some protection for the plants.

There was always a problem to be solved or worked out, and the couple bounced things off each other for their solutions. "Where are we going to get water once the bottled water we got at the *Superbodega* and the mini-markets runs out?" Alicia asked one evening as they sat by candle light.

Immediately after 'the incident' David and Alicia knew that they would not have an immediate problem obtaining fresh water for drinking and cooking. The stores were full of bottled water, and David soon discovered that the national brewery, about seven miles away, was also the franchisee for one of the major international soft-drink companies and distributed huge tanks of bottled water for use in office coolers. But how long would that last?

It also was rainy season which meant no scarcity of daily fresh water…at least until the dry season arrived in mid-November. David responded with some certainty, "I think I should be able to tap the down spouts on our building. And there are always the neighboring buildings to drain water into barrels and other containers. The problem will be if I have enough time to get it done before the rainy season ends. There is still a lot to be done in the garden plots."

Alicia responded with a simple, "Humm." In her mind she was thinking, *"So many things to think about, worry about and solve. It is hard work to just survive…and in such crazy circumstances."* Both of them had a lot of time either in the garden or at home to think by themselves. And for Alicia thoughts constantly swirled in her head.

She thought about their adult children. If there was no one on the radio or ham broadcasts that

David had sent out that first night, then their kids had likely not survived. Both of the kids had learned at an early age to run a ham radio and had their own sets and licenses. However, they realized that there was no electricity to send or receive messages. And they seemed to be the sole survivors.

They had the will to live, but how long would that resolve remain? They had no friends or colleagues left. People are social beings, and though she was so grateful David too had survived, how were they going to manage on just each other's company? How they missed being in the classroom and the relationships they had through work and church.

When they both worked, they would come home with so much to share with each other. That was the basis of their good relationship, a close friendship. They were always glad to meet up and tell one another about their day. They would talk for hours on everything from politics to contacts they had had from their kids by email to gossip from work. But how long could they sustain a conversation about a garden or canning vegetables?

They did have lots to remember, trips, previous locations and the experiences in those places. But would that get a little old? How many times could they listen to some of the same stories from their growing up years? Would life be all work and no play from this point on?

Another thought that popped into her head was, "*Should they keep a calendar, a log of activities or a journal? Would anyone be interested someday. Ever?*

So many questions and in many cases, no easy answers.

There were times when her fears overwhelmed her. Yes, she had a deep faith and was told from early Sunday school classes that she was not to worry, but, it was a little difficult when it appeared you were the only ones on earth. Would snakes overtake the neighborhood? Would they pick up any diseases from all the bodies decaying in the homes around them?

They had resolved in their minds the fact that all of the laws and ethics of a normal day had flown out the window and no longer applied. They no longer found it difficult to steal from a neighbor's home or from another mini-market they ran across in their rounds of a neighborhood. They more easily went around bodies lying on the sidewalks or even on the streets. The worst part of that was the fact that the flesh had not stopped smelling. They knew that would go away with time, but they were not exactly up to date on such information and had no place to look…even the library likely did not have a book on such a subject. If they did, it would be the least checked out book they ever shelved. Would they look up, "How long does it take for a human body to decompose?" Or, "How long will the human body smell after it dies?" Just the thought of such questions disgusted Alicia, but under the circumstances she wouldn't mind knowing just how long they would they have to tolerate these things.

Thoughts constantly swirled in her head, and though they had been too busy to talk much about it, she decided David likely had the same thoughts repeating themselves in his head. How many nights had he not gone to sleep trying to resolve a problem? Too many for Alicia to count.

While David spent much of each day at the various gardens or going for supplies, Alicia had her own work challenges to surmount. After they had achieved entry to several neighboring houses, she set about cleaning rooms out in preparation to use them as warehouses. She stored goods that they brought from various stores, making note of what was where and working to secure those buildings from wild animals. Assuring that nothing would spoil or disintegrate was impossible, but she worked at it to the best of her ability.

She also researched medical books and scavenged the storage supplies of a local hospital as well as several pharmacies for medicines and other items that they might need. She was so glad she had brought with them a book called, *Where There is no Doctor*. It was essential reading material for those going to the remote jungles of the world and mighty helpful for them right now.

As they brought home some of the initial fresh fruit, she prepared them for storage by canning them in bottles that they found at the *Super Ferreteria*. Though she had canned when she and David first married, with all the fresh stuff available in Costa Brava there had been no reason to do it. Every country they had lived in had a bi-weekly or weekly market with wonderful fresh products. But now with the help of an old cookbook that had a section about canning, it became a necessity.

From the beginning, the couple recognized their need to grow and store food and obtain sufficient water for survival day to day and year-round. This consumed them for months.

Some of the technical challenges weren't as easy.

Chapter 12

The technical problems and necessities challenged David the most. After all, he was an academic. But he wasn't someone with a great deal of technical or mechanical knowledge or ability. Long ago he had figured out which end of the hammer to hold and how to change a lamp plug or hang a picture on the wall or how to change the innards of a balky toilet. But to re-engineer a house or add plumbing or an alternative electric system was way beyond his field of knowledge. He knew that would have to change for them to survive.

Their son, when he was a teenager, thought his dad was a total loser when it came to doing things that were technical. He once commented about that.

"Do you remember that short story that Rich wrote when he was taking a writing class in college?" David asked.

"He wrote a lot. Which one are you referring to?"

"The one where his friend's father could do just about anything, and his couldn't do anything short of hold a hammer right." he replied to her question.

"Oh yes, do I! But remember how he ended it?"

David interrupted her before she could tell the ending. "He decided that his dad had some attributes that his friend's dad didn't have…ability to write and his leadership abilities…and wasn't so bad after all." They both smiled.

They need this lighter moment in the midst of such a heavy time and monumental change in their lives. But, a heaviness fell over them both as they realized that their son was likely not even alive. They moved on in silence, each with their own thoughts.

From the moment the electricity went out they were without power, except by using generators, for refrigeration or lights or entertainment. Fortunately they used tanks of bottled gas for their stove and there were thousands of those around town on trucks and in various warehouses or *bodegas*.

David began first to solve the water supply problem. Though water was ever present in a country of tropical downpours and rushing rivers, the problem was that ninety-five percent of the rain came in the seven to eight-month rainy season, leaving them with four or five months of saving water from occasional afternoon thunderstorms, storing it, or hauling it from a nearby river or pond.

"Why couldn't we go after one of those tanks that collect water on the roof?" Alicia asked when they were discussing it. "I have seen those blue ones in all sizes."

"Yes, but they are huge. How would we get it here? We would have to find one that would fit into the truck we commandeered at beginning of all this."

After a few moments, he continued, "And how do I connect it up? I think it needs a reservoir at the bottom and then the water has to be pumped up. So, it will require the generators to do that, and we both know the gasoline to run them will give out with time."

"Well, first you might solve both problems if we wander into the area where you could buy one. And we can see what we are contending with."

"Yup. You have a point there." David conceded. "Why worry about something we haven't the foggiest idea about yet. Did you ever look at the hundreds... thousands... on rooftops and think we would be installing one for our water supply?"

"Yeah, you're right. Until you need them, they're *just there*. I can't say that I have ever seen one installed. Have you?" Alicia commented.

"We are not installing one on the roof, but on the ground. Hopefully that is a bit easier."

Alice jumped right in with, "Lifting one up to the roof would be a lot worse without the equipment or the knowledge as to how to do it. One way or another, I think it is going to be a two person job."

"Yes. This is one thing I can't handle without your help"

Within a week David and Alicia began to tackle these issues. They made plans to go out for what they needed to install some type of cistern rigged from the rooftop tanks, and came back with the first of several with which to experiment. Why drag lots of big plastic containers until they found out what it would take to install one?

With adequate water supply in rainy season David quickly set up temporary barrels at the bottom of some of the down spouts which he crudely tied in to their shower and sinks and toilets. As time permitted with still working on the garden for a food supply, he added some more barrels, as well as the large tank they procured, behind their house for storage and placed more tanks next to neighboring buildings. For the first six months they used bottled water from the supermarket and the local distillery.

Gasoline for transportation was another question. Every car around the city had some gas in it and the government-owned petroleum company had the odd practice of parking the huge tanker delivery trucks at gas stations overnight. So, initially they had plenty of gasoline supply to keep a fleet of cars and pick-up trucks running which facilitated getting around the city. And, they hoped when the work of getting set up ended, they would go on occasional day or weekend trips out into the countryside. They were too busy with work and adjustments however. That would come with time.

The real question was how to get the gasoline out of the tanker, plus, how long it would be usable. "Always a problem." David muttered out loud, more to himself than to Alicia who had gone with him as she did on most excursions.

David had heard that gasoline had a shelf life or a tank usability of up to one year. But reading some material he found at the university library, he discovered that gasoline in a tank, like a truck, could remain useful for up to three years but in a car's carburetor system it might gum up within three months. He realized he would have to run each of the vehicles they had accumulated regularly to work the gas through the carburetor. On the other hand, David discovered that diesel fuel might remain good for up to two years.

Every evening, by candlelight they talked.

"Does it all seem overwhelming to you David?" Alicia remarked. "I mean do you ever get the feeling that it might not be worth it? I am already lonely. Don't misunderstand me, I am so glad for your company, but do you realize we will never see anyone but each other again?'

David sat for a few seconds before he responded. "Yes. I think about what you just said many times as I am pulling weeds or planting seeds in our plots. It isn't easy, I know. But the alternative is to just give up and I am not ready to do that. I feel so fortunate to get the things we have accumulated since the 'incident' and know it has to get easier with time"

David had always been the one to come up with a more positive thought or a good *other-side-of-the-coin*-response. Through the years Alicia had observed David at meetings. He would not say a word for quite a while. Then his hand would go slowly up, even as others were finishing what they had to say. And in one sentence he could shed new light on the situation and bring it all together. It would often be the consensus in the end.

When the two were talking at home, he could do the same thing. He was always the more positive one after Alicia had come up with all the problems or negatives. Bingo, he nailed it.

"You're right David. But I just have not gotten over the grieving process, for the kids, friends, the normal way of life, the lively productive lives we lived for so many years that we enjoyed so much."

She paused and thought for a moment. "No, giving up is not an option. But poof, the normal is all gone. I used to hate the term, *new normal* just like you hate the words, *safety is our highest priority* when a company has done something that has injured a lot of people. But *new normal* is the only way to describe this strange situation. Hopefully, we will both feel a little better with time, but with some of these changes, maybe never."

The conversation shifted as it always did each evening to another problem or situation to be solved.

Soon, he set to work creating alternative power sources for light, the water heater, washing clothes and eventually entertainment. Yet, at the same time they began to adjust to *not* having some of these things. The couple knew they would eventually have to move to another source of electric power other than generators to meet their various needs. Having had a long time interest in environmental issues they decided that solar and possibly wind power was their easiest and most reliable source of alternative generation of power. But…where to get the supplies for wind? Maybe solar would not be so difficult as more and more homeowners were taking advantage of the plentiful sun.

He was always amazed to see the ingenious ways people tapped into the sun's power. One that intrigued him was at Alicia's and his favorite restaurant up on the mountain. They would go for special occasions, arriving early enough to explore the extensive, beautiful, varied and relaxing gardens. The restaurant was in a hotel complex that also had cabins. The cottages were fitted with large black hoses curled neatly on the roof in a circular way. They were held in place with what looked like spokes of a wagon wheel, starting at the hub and going out. It was obvious to David that as the water sat in the black hose it heated and likely fed into a heater so it could be topped off on a series of cloudy days, but otherwise probably quite adequate for normal use.

After talking about it one evening, David said, "I think I will try to get some hot water into the house using the circular black hoses like we saw on the roofs of the cabins at the Bougenvilla Hotel. What do you think?"

"Well, what I think is you're not doing that! Just how do you expect to get up on the roof of this building to get the hose up there? No. No. No, David. Think again," Alicia responded.

"Hmmm. Not such a good idea, huh. Can you think of a better idea?" he asked with a little irritation in his voice.

It didn't take but a couple of seconds for her response. "Down at the beach, we saw small metal tanks painted black that supplied hot water to the showers in the rooms. Is there any way to find one around town attach it to the side of the building? It won't be the most aesthetic thing, but it might work.

"Aesthetics might be the least of our worries right now. But we still have to get the water to the window level," he quipped.

You could attach it with braces and you would not have to go to the roof and kill yourself. I would prefer to keep you in one piece with no broken bones, if you don't mind."

"Well, I am all for the 'no broken bones' and 'not kill yourself' parts. It could work, but we will have to search out small metal tanks--ones that are not too heavy, and then the braces to hang them. Maybe a hook type thing would work."

"Then, off to *Super Ferriteria*, right? Tomorrow?"

"No. Let's save a bit of fuel and get a longer list together. Hot water may not be our biggest need at the moment, and besides, maybe we will figure a way to get the water into a tank. Maybe there is a hand pump that will do it. I don't know until I look around"

"Always the practical one", Alicia thought. "Sounds like a good plan."

So they added the materials to a list they were making for their next 'shopping trip' and moved on to the next subject, having at least worked out a plan of sorts.

David had seen some advertisements in the local newspaper for solar power. In addition, he and Alicia had visited a solar powered house at an ecological park in the city. At one point they even considered moving to the park to live in the already-constructed alternative powered house. However, they soon recognized that they had already started the gardens near their present home and they appreciated the panoramic view that they had from their living room window, so they decided to stay put.

After visiting the park, David was able to note how the solar panels were installed. The project began.

Gathering the things they needed was not such an easy task, but decided to start small to not be overwhelmed. The set-up required storage batteries, the panels, the wiring, and a lot of other things. It seemed like it would be fairly easy, but brought enough teamwork, frustrations, snippy conversations and "discussion" between them to last a long time. But when it was all done, there was a huge sense of accomplishment. And, with written material available in the information center, they were able to add a system to their building within a few months that generated most of their limited electric needs.

Being frugal, the couple limited their electrical usage to basic lighting at night, refrigeration and later a small chest freezer and the occasional use of entertainment equipment including a CD player for music and DVD players for their television. Gone was the need for computers, radios and other technological equipment such as telephones. Within six months they were able to supply their limited power needs completely

"Let's go hunting for some DVD's that we haven't seen yet." Alicia suggested. So, one day, when they thought they could spare the time, they took off for their usual library source for things in English. They were excited about their huge pile of new material to view that they carried up the stairs to their apartment.

Next, David tackled a more permanent water supply system for their home. Using a forklift taken from the *Super Ferretería*, they installed a large tank in the yard next to theirs. From there David ran plumbing (assisted by a small water pump powered by their solar panels) to a roof top storage tank that acted as a pressurized delivery system to the house. A Rube Goldberg system of drains and pipes brought in water not only from their house but two adjoining homes, assuring them of an adequate supply for most of the year. Later he brought in an additional tank for more storage and a back-up in case the first tank failed.

"You know Hon, having a car and other vehicles we have commandeered has been a real blessing," David commented one day as they rested after a long day of work.

"I agree David, but I've been thinking that we can't count on them forever," Alicia reflected. "Sooner or later they will break down, or the gasoline supply will run out or go bad and we will be without any of those vehicles you have collected around the neighborhood and at the mall parking lot."

"Oh, I know that," David agreed. "I've been thinking about that. So, tomorrow I think that we ought to go golfing."

"David!" Alicia exclaimed. "What are you talking about?

"Oh, you'll see my love. Want to go with me tomorrow?"

"I don't know," she replied. "Sometimes I think I just ought to stay home."

The next morning the couple drove the fifteen miles to the upscale golf club that they had visited with friends once or twice. It was a favorite haunt of Marcella, a close friend who had come to the country right after college to teach and had stayed, rising up through the ranks at the same university where they taught.

Now retired but continuing to live in Costa Brava, Marcella enjoyed meeting friends over lunch before taking to the golf links before the afternoon thunderstorm sent her heading home. It was her place and her way of socializing without having to do all of the cooking and cleaning that she detested.

"It seems funny to come out here and not expect to see Marcella meeting us at the door," Alicia complained as she entered the club's driveway. The lack of contact with other people was beginning to take its toll, more each passing day.

"This is the part that is the hardest here. We had so many good friends…so many good friends…." Her voice trailed off to silence as they pulled up to the now-dirty red carpet that led into the clubhouse restaurant.

Looking out over what had been a super-manicured golf course, she teared up as she saw tall weeds, fallen trees, blown-in litter and general disarray over the once pristine area.

David drove right on by the large double doors and pulled up into the no-parking zone at the entrance to the golf course.

Hopping out, he directed Alicia toward the golf cart rental office. "What a great supply of transportation! But don't you have to charge them with electricity."

David just grinned and, taking her arm, walked her over to the line of at least twenty-five vehicles lined up along the edge of the course.

"Up there, look up there," David said pointing to the top of several carts.

Alicia just stared. "Of course," she exclaimed. "David, you are so smart. I never considered that some of these carts were solar powered. Of course, we can travel—well—forever with these!"

David went back to the office and quickly broke in the door. Looking around behind the counter, he found a key rack with over two-dozen sets of cart keys hanging in neat organized numerical order to match each appropriate cart.

Carrying several sets of keys, David jumped into the first cart and cranked the starter. Immediately the electric motor sparked to life. David grinned at Alicia and said, "Hop aboard."

Over the following several weeks David and Alicia brought home several of the carts, parking some of them at the parking garage at the mall for weather protection and to avoid too much congestion around their house. They eventually brought home one six-passenger cart which they might find very useful later.

Bit by bit they added to their huge fleet of transportation, technical equipment and capability, gradually easing their life style.

Meanwhile, around them, they watched with fascination as the city changed, slowly but surely. Initially, the air cleared and continued to be fresh, tropical and pleasing. The water in the river ebbed and flowed with the coming and going of the annual rainy and dry seasons, but after six months they noticed a definite reduction not only in the amount of trash that flowed through but in the pollution of the water itself. Now, it was much clearer and the number of fish seemed to be increasing a bit. Trash continued to blow around, but seemed to diminish as it decomposed or became lodged in ditches or against buildings.

Vegetation increased everywhere, grass sprouting up through cracks, vines all over the trees and invading the roadways, narrowing the boulevard close to them from four lanes to two. Cars along the way began to cover with vines and rust and fall apart.

From time to time they saw and heard birds that they had never seen before or had viewed only in zoos or rural areas. Wild dogs continued to roam the streets and present a threat, but stray cats had all but disappeared. Occasional troops of monkeys would pass through the neighborhood, swinging from trees, stealing their precious bananas and other fruits.

Perhaps they too had changed, though they had not noticed too much even when they looked in the mirrors at home. But things like haircuts and shaves more often went by the wayside. Clothes were slowly wearing out and harder to wash, and comforts they had long enjoyed were also gone. Conversations were totally different from before the incident had occurred. One evening Alicia blurted out, "What do you miss the most now, David?"

It did not take long for his response. "Without a doubt still having other people around. Don't take me wrong I am so glad you are here, but no social life has been so hard."

"Yes, I agree, but at times I miss the strangest things. The constant buzz of other people around, working and the comradery at the "U" and I even miss traffic and the driving pattern."

"For me it is the challenge of finding what you want, exploring new areas of town, but another big one for me is the church and the fellowship."

They sat silently for a while until Alicia started to reminisce about the diversity of an international church. "How many countries do you think were represented at the San Juan Union Church?"

"When we lived in Thailand there were 35," she added. "Remember that international service where about 10 people read the same scripture in their language and the countries were listed as people stood to tell where they were from?"

David chimed in, "It was so cool. Now to your question about the church here", and he hesitated a few seconds before jumping back to Alicia's question, "I think maybe 20 countries were represented. It was a small congregation compared to the Thailand church."

"One of the most exciting parts was meeting people from every English speaking part of the world, as well as having some local people whose English was so good that they preferred to worship in English," Alicia added.

Alicia was not the only one with a sad face and a few tears ready to roll down her face. David was having a hard time as well as he tried to be strong and manly.

The couple got used to lots of things about their new life, but never the loneliness of not having other humans around. Church had been one of their main times of social interaction. They might enjoy time to themselves, but the constant time together with no other contact took major adjustment for each of them.

They moved closer together on the sofa and stared out the window, comforting each other.

Yes, life became easier and more comfortable in many ways…that is, until one night a disaster threatened to take away everything they had and worked so hard to accomplish. Little did they realize that once again their lives would change and they would have to make more adaptations.

Chapter 13

Ten years later.

This time it wasn't the silence that awoke David. It was the noise, a tremendous roar that shook the house and woke both of them instantly-an explosion like no other they had experienced.

"David, what was that?" Alicia asked, almost screaming, as she reacted to the loud boom and the apartment shaking.

"I'm not sure Hon."

The two jumped up, and is the practice in earthquake-prone areas, immediately slipped on their shoes which they kept by the bed in case they had to escape over broken glass that would cut their feet. Rushing to the front double windows they looked out over the central valley of Costa Brava, their hearts pounding from the fright, their breathing rapid.

As usual, there was little to see. They had never again seen a light across the valley since "the incident" though at times they looked out longingly for some other sign of human life. It was a clear night with no moon, thus the stars were even brighter than usual. The loud explosions came periodically with the sound bouncing off distant mountains and reverberating in the valley until it died a slow death. Then for a moment or two there was silence before the next violent crack or thunder-like uproar.

Then they saw it.

"Look, David, oh my gosh!" exclaimed Alicia as she pointed to Izkatzu Volcano, a good 30 miles away. "Look at that!"

Now there was no doubt of the origin of the noise that was bouncing around as it hit various land features or buildings.

David's mouth dropped open as he surveyed the incredible scene in front of him. The mountain, dormant for nearly 100 years, according to volcanologists from the University of Costa Brava, had sprung to life in front of their eyes. Despite the darkness, they could see the huge mushroom of ash and debris rising miles into the sky. Lightening flashed within the huge pyroclastic cloud and the mountain's lower flanks were illuminated by the glow of lava as it streamed down the sides of the mountain.

Long red rivers of the molten lava now snaked down the mountainside with red rocks tumbling below, setting fire to grass, trees and ruined buildings. And, moving ever closer toward them.

"David, do you think we are safe here?" Alicia asked with a tremble of fear in her voice.

"Yeah, I think so," he answered, putting his arm around her waist to comfort her. "After all, we are 30 miles away and for now I think that we have seen the biggest blast. Not that there won't be more smaller ones, but much of the energy is spent and now it will need to cool down and we will have to see whether another lava dome builds or whether it has blown itself out for another century."

After this short discussion about their safety, which included discussing how far the destroyed communities were to Mt. Vesuvius in Italy in ancient times, they were not sure, but decided they were further away than the communities buried in ash after that eruption.

As things quieted, they both felt a little calmer as they realized they were not in immediate danger of lava overtaking their house, or of the lightning setting the area on fire.

"It is awesome to watch, isn't it? It's like natural fireworks," David finally said in a much calmer voice.

"Yes, but I could still do without this. It reminds me of the times we watched some pretty awesome lightning storms from our condo in Miami," Alicia put in.

Then David had a thought. "How many times did we try to see the active volcano Ariana in the middle of Costa Brava when we went up to hot pools and the lake near that volcano with Pablo and Maria? It was either cloudy or rainy or foggy. Now we have our own show without even leaving our apartment."

"Humm. Yes, but really I would prefer to have Pablo and Maria back…if I had a choice between a volcano or friends…" and her voice trailed off without finishing her sentence. It had been a little while since these close friends had come up in a conversation. It was a bit easier to mention them, but the pain was far from completely gone even after all this time. She was jolted from her reverie by another loud explosion that rattled the windows in the apartment.

Even at this distance they could begin to smell the acid sulfuric smoke and soon sensed what they at first thought was a snowfall.

"Ash," David exclaimed. "That's volcanic ash that's falling, Hon."

Alicia quickly closed the windows to keep the bulk of it from filtering into their apartment. Then she ran for wet towels to put along the bottom of the doorway to the porch. Despite her efforts, some of the dust seeped into the apartment and began to lay a thin layer across the tables and floors.

Stunned by what was taking place in front of their eyes, the couple held hands and watched as the ash cloud reached higher altitudes where the wind began to stretch it out and blow it toward the ocean.

Below, the flow of pyroclastic rock continued to be thrown in the air like a cork from a champagne bottle with all its fizz and spray. It flowed over the rim of the mountain's crater as well and down the sides.

"The high-altitude winds are blowing the cloud out to sea and most of the lava seems to be flowing off to the north," David observed. "So other than some of the ash that is being blown this way by the lower wind, everything seems to be moving away from us."

In a sense, they weren't surprised by the blast, though its size and force startled them. For several months the frequency and intensity of temblors and actual, outright earthquakes had been increasing giving them some uneasy days with their slightly swaying building and noise of items falling in apartments now unoccupied. And, they had noticed more of the wisps of smoke that occasionally arose from the mountain's crater. In fact, in the past few weeks the smoke from the crater had been more intense and thicker than they had noticed before.

Until dawn David and Alicia sat together on the couch in front of their picture window watching the natural fireworks on the other side of the valley. Occasionally they would hear a rumble as another explosion rocked the huge mountain and set off a waterfall of red, molten material.

David and Alicia were not convinced that engineering in Costa Brava was quite up to standards of other parts of the world or that the quality of materials, like cement, was stable enough. Yet they had lived in places with worse reputations for building standards and codes. The code might exist, but with a little money under the table to the contractor , it might be enough to move forward with construction.

Many a time they had felt the apartment building where they lived roll a bit in an earthquake, or they heard glass break with a huge crash in someone's house nearby. There was nothing as unnerving as feeling you were moving with a slight up and down motion, or to hear the deep rumble of a moving building.

Even the apartment building they were in made them nervous despite the fact it that had withstood a couple of good shakers. Perhaps it was a testament to the two fine men, owners of the structure, who had told them of overseeing the construction work to assure their own and other occupant's safety.

They had been in a store where the shelves rocked back and forth. They had done what they needed to do in that situation; gone to the entrance, leaving their grocery cart behind, until the quake or tremors stopped. When it was all over, they would return to finish grabbing a few important things, paying for their goods, leaving as soon as they could

One major earthquake had put a huge crack in the side of a three story, half-block department store in downtown San Juan. When they went to the center of the city a few weeks later on an errand, they looked up to see scaffolding. Men were just filling in the crack, rather than shore up the building or really repair it. At the time they just shook their head. But they had to admit that it was still standing years later, despite what they considered shoddy repair work.

In fact, the excellent construction of the building the couple was in was just one of the reasons that they had stayed in their smaller apartment rather than to re-locate to a larger house in a more upscale neighborhood after the initial incident that killed everyone else.

They considered their familiarity with the apartment, the neighborhood, the nearby resources for obtaining needed goods to be essential.

Yes, other houses might have been more opulent, but their apartment was somehow "just right" in many ways. Moreover, they decided that as the last people on earth--as far as they were able to determine--they wouldn't want to lose each other or become strangers in an overly-large house. They needed each other close by more than ever, still reeling from loneliness and lack of social contact.

As the sun rose from behind the mountain the couple was startled by the diffused light that spread slowly across the valley. And, they were surprised that most of the rich tropical green that they took for granted everywhere was gone. In its place trees, bushes, roofs, grass--everything was coated with a thin layer of volcanic ash that had fallen throughout the night. It appeared that they had suddenly been thrust into winter. Everything seemed to be covered by snow, just like David experienced as a kid growing up in northeast Ohio or that he and Alicia had experienced the winter that they spent teaching at the university in Prague. Lawns, roofs, sidewalks, trees, all sported this thin covering of what, at second look, appeared to be more like dirty snow.

With the approach of a new day, the couple noticed that the clouds of dust and ash from the volcano were diminishing. In the sunlight they were not able to gauge the flow of lava, but they had noticed fewer rivulets of the material flowing in the last hour before dawn and the occasional explosions had ceased.

Finally, they began to stir. They did not realize that they had gone to sleep sitting on the sofa and resting up against each other.

"I must be really tired. I fell asleep, even with the rumbling," David mumbled in his usual morning stupor. And Alicia agreed taking a final look outside before quickly popping up to prepare their morning coffee and tea, and David slowly dressed to take an outdoor survey.

"*A hard day in front of us,*" she thought with an audible sigh. And, apparently David was thinking the same thing, because he too let out a sigh. Then in his usual way he began to make plans as to what to tackle first of another monumental crisis.

They decided not to change their clothes. They were going to have a lot of dirty work ahead of them, and after all, they had not seen any other human beings in nearly eight years. The various dogs, cattle and occasional monkeys that roamed the neighborhood seemed generally oblivious to their existence and even the parrots that chattered on the nearby roofs seemed more interested in communicating with each other than with them.

Perhaps out of habit if nothing else, each day both of them followed their life-long habits of wearing bed clothes at night and work clothes during the day. They even continued to "dress up" on Sunday when they took time for a private Bible study and worship or when they decided to take a trip somewhere to picnic in the mountains or in a nearby park. Somehow, they found, keeping their old habits and rhythms helped them to cope with the daily routine of survival and the lack of social contact other than with each other. And, though life was certainly better now than in the early days, routines continued to be comforting.

His quick survey trip in the yard of their apartment building and around the neighborhood was eerily reminiscent of that day nearly a decade ago when their lives changed suddenly and forever.

That same morning he had left their apartment to explore the strange silence that they experienced. That day he took the same route that he took this day, down the block, up the hill and left toward the park, now totally overgrown with time. Then, left at the main street, also changed with time, and to the mall.

Thankfully there were no new bodies or unexpected surprises. They did not need either of those things at this point in their lives. Once was enough. Getting used to all the changes when they found so many bodies and realized only they had survived whatever it was that had caused everyone to disappear took time. Any idea of having to go through another trauma was not exactly appealing to them. The difference this time was this catastrophe was identifiable, where the previous one was never settled in their minds. That did not stop them from thinking about it and discussing it.

The irony was that in spite of the snowy appearance, the weather was still tropical warm and the trees and bushes were still in full leaf.

"*At least the ash fall isn't too thick*," David mused as he turned the corner at the mall and headed back home uneasy, but not alarmed by what he saw.

Alicia had decided that they needed something to break the routine, so prepared a hearty breakfast and piled on the food. Their conversation was totally about the explosions and the work ahead of them.

Some low rumbles continued, but nothing to stop them from starting to clean up mess created by the ash.

Then, with her help he climbed on the roof, something that he had avoided at Alecia's encouragement for a long time. But he had commandeered a long extension ladder from the local fire department, and he felt it was sturdier and safer, and she agreed finally. Her words as he began his ascent were always the same, "Be careful. I worry about you when you go up on the roof." And though he reassured her, she would not be relaxed until he was safely on the ground.

He didn't want to put too much extra weight on the building. Stories in the newspapers of the past always talked about this or that building that had collapsed under the weight of ash. Another one told of the new local management who did not understand why the foreigners from whom they had purchased the company were always cleaning the cement dust from the roof. After a good rain, they knew. The building roof caved in, creating a shortage of cement until they could get up and running. They had laughed at the foreigners until that fateful day. He was not interested in chancing that with ash on the apartment building.

He carefully swept all the ash, loading it into buckets that he lowered to Alecia to empty in the side of their lot.

He was no longer worried about cement forming or rain drains clogging.

"I think I better clean the solar panels while I am up there. I won't be any longer than I have to. We have to check the gardens and animals for damage as soon as possible," he called down to her as he walked around the roof.

The job done, he climbed down and put the ladder back in its safe place. David's trip to the roof went as well as can be expected, though he came down exhausted by the work, but also with a deep sense of satisfaction. Though ten years had passed since "the incident," and he was older, David felt the way hard work had toned his muscles, but he still wasn't getting any younger!

"I am so glad that is over for us," Alicia said with an obvious tone of relief in her voice, concerned for David's safety as much as anything.

"I am just as glad it's over. That was hard work!" was the best reply he could give.

With time the rains would wash some of the ash from the plants around their apartment building, or the leaves would drop off and it would not be long before new ones would sprout out. But, the garden had to be cleaned off as soon as possible before it blocked out sun which would limit growth or kill the plants. Their existence depended on those vegetables as well as the ash covered fruit trees.

It all meant more work for them, and secretly they were both inwardly moaned at the extra labor this ash had created.

The chickens, cows and plants could not survive this layer of caustic ash and needed to be washed off. They knew from basic earth science when they studied volcanos in grammar school that ash could carry potentially poisonous chemicals that neither they nor the animals could survive.

Even micro-organisms living in soil couldn't survive, and trees or their limbs broke under the weight, much the same as ice in northern states during or after an ice storm. Though volcanic soil can be very rich for some plants nearer to the eruption site, David and Alicia were not close enough to that, they thankfully agreed, to benefit from this new richness. In time they would see plants making a comeback; that is if they were closer.

Conscience of the danger to their lungs, they took precautions by making a mask from an old T-shirt. They hoped that was sufficient to keep the crystals in the ash from damaging the delicate tissue in their lungs.

"We'll share the work on the animals and garden. I'm glad you are willing to go up on that roof. I just couldn't handle that," Alicia volunteered with a slight shiver to her shoulders.

"I'm not big on it either, but it can't be left. I will be glad for your help with the garden and critters."

With each rain and wind, they would hear a new set of sounds. The first time startled both of them. As they sat reading during the usual *siesta* storm, there suddenly was a loud crack close by that froze them in their place.

"What was that?" she asked look up with a look of alarm from her reading "I can guarantee it was not thunder."

Warily and with a cold chill, David responded, "I don't know."

It didn't take long for curiosity that outweighed the fear to make him jump to his feet. His first glance out the front window gave him his answer. To the left of their apartment was a huge old tree that had blown across the street with the weight of the ash and rain, crushing the house next to them, throwing some of the debris against the windowless wall of their downstairs apartment/storage rooms. The street was obviously totally blocked off in that direction.

"Do you suppose we are trapped in this block with a tree on the other side?"

By the time David could answer, she was on her feet, standing next to him. "I can't see anything from here. We at least won't have a huge tree to cut down, though we will have to get used to coming and going from the one entrance to our street."

The tree blocking one way to their building was really a small price to pay compared to what might have happened if the wind had been blowing just a bit more from the left. They were safe, though shaken, and still able to get to some things they had stored in the neighbor's now crushed house. They spent parts of several days moving the things stored there to their now increasing space as things were used up or had to be thrown out because of rot, rust, mold, mildew or just age.

Over the years David and Alicia had accustomed themselves to living with unfettered nature in the tropics. Without city crews to keep the roads clear and the parks trimmed and without neighbors to keep their own yards under control, the city was beginning to look like one of those movies relating to what happens to the earth after all human life stops. It reminded them of photos of the famous overgrown ruins in Peru when they were first discovered years after the people had abandoned their city on the mountain top.

Soon after the recent volcanic eruption, Costa Brava began to look denuded, showing a network of leafless vines and empty tree branches. It would not take long however to grow back up, as a rainforest quickly rejuvenates.

Most obvious, weeks after the incident, were lawns and empty lots that had grown wild and were returning to their original rain forest status. Even trees had grown up in abandoned house gutters or any place they could take hold, and cracks wove their way on streets and parking lots with tall grasses, while vines crept up the sides of buildings and were starting to obscure some houses and stores creating grotesque images that resembled giant green ghosts.

General debris, falling leaves and branches and other free-blowing trash had accumulated along the curbs of street and were pushed into the sewer lines by the torrential tropical rains. As a result, in many places sewer grates were blocked and water backed up in the streets during a hard rain…at least until paper or cardboard could disintegrate. Soon mud flowed into the drains as well.

Buildings definitely showed neglect. Since most painters' first step in Costa Brava was to water down the otherwise good quality paint to make it go further, most surfaces had lost their cover in the intervening years. Now, bare wood was rotting and at times falling off of buildings. Gutters hung at angles as their supports broke off under the weight of dirt and leaves that filled them.

Many roofs had lost their tiles as water seeped in underneath and was not stopped. Leaks were expanding. Occasional earthquakes and windstorms had broken many windows around town so that a variety of wildlife was now living in many formerly plush living rooms. Water blowing or leaking in was creating further damage and instability. Their own apartment on the top floor was no exception, with the paint getting dull, small leaks needing to be taken care of immediately. They circled all the properties they were using to pick up debris and fallen branches.

Never having considered himself as a handyman, David found keeping the house maintained to be a real challenge. He much preferred to be in the gardens weeding, planting or harvesting the various crops. Much more, he wanted to mow lawns or clean up the streets rather than to face the challenge of maintaining a house, climbing up on the roof or trying to keep the solar-powered generators going.

The two kind landlords who owned their apartment would be mortified if they could see the building so many years after everything changed, because they had kept the building in top shape.

David and Alicia had about all they could handle to obtain their food supply. So the building received care, but not as the owners would have done.

Once, the condition of the building prompted Alicia to say, "Do you suppose it is a blessing that the landlords did not make it out of this whole event that killed off everyone?"

"It is horrible to say, but maybe you are right. They were fastidious, weren't they?"

"Can you imagine the reaction people would have if they came alive and saw the condition of their house or apartment building as it is today? This was always such a nice neighborhood, despite litter and a few other things. But look at it today," Alicia said finishing off her ramblings. And, all David could do was to agree.

Going back to their own thoughts, Alicia began wondering about people coming back to life after all these years. *"Could I adjust to other people anymore? We have lived alone. Would I want to share what we have with others? Would I want to work at the university anymore? What if our children came back?"*

"I suppose it would depend on who came back; a casual acquaintance or Pedro and Maria or the kids." Our kids and closest friends yes, but others? I'm not so sure anymore."

Not wanting to share her thoughts, she did not ask David if he too thought about such things. They both knew by now that people coming back wasn't going to happen. However, they were thoughts she had from time to time.

While the plant kingdom was enjoying unchecked growth, expanding where it wanted, the animal kingdom wasn't suffering either.

In the early days, David and Alicia had noted the pitiable condition of domesticated pets that were wandering the streets. Having two cats from the Von Boems, as well as their own, they felt they had enough pets to care for without taking on a city full of stray cats or even dogs for that matter. Furthermore, they tried, with only modest success, to pen and maintain the cows that wandered the neighborhood and some chickens they housed in a yard a few blocks away. The milk and eggs were useful to balance their diet. Neither considered themselves particularly agricultural people, especially as far as taking care of animals was concerned, but after Alicia took a few books from the university's agriculture studies department, they learned enough to reap the benefits. Husbandry was not their forte, but then, other things were out of their previous realm as well.

Dogs were a serious problem for the first few years. Many died trapped behind garden walls or inside of their owner's homes, but others escaped and joined up with the plethora of wild dogs present on the streets in so many developing countries. Hungry, and probably frightened, some became vicious, often charging David or Alicia if they were on the streets. This made it necessary to carry some sort of defense. Trips out meant automatically grabbing a walking stick. Though they did not like the idea of killing strays, it was a matter of safety, and they had to do so at times. They knew that rabid dogs would mean a slow death, and they were working hard to survive. Not all cat and dog owners in Costa Brava were as conscientious as the Von Boems, making sure that their feline's shots were up to date.

For his own protection, David also started to carry a gun when he went outside of their yard to work in the gardens or seek supplies at another location. In time, he built wooden fences around the gardens to keep marauding animals out, protecting both himself and the crops. Eventually, the previously domesticated animals, like dogs and cats, reverted to their original wild nature and learned to forage and hunt for food. When the danger from dogs seemed to be passed and they moved to these wild, primitive locations away from them, he and Alicia were certain that there were no other human beings who might be a threat. So David stopped carrying the gun.

Wild animals, meanwhile, quickly adapted and enjoyed the lack of human predators in what had originally been their habitat. Within months Alicia commented that she was seeing more birds and a different variety of species than what they had seen before. In the gardens and local parks, David noticed an increase in some animals he did not know grew in Costa Brava.

"Aren't the changes we have seen the last little while amazing? Everything from the advancing vegetation to the domestic animals readapting to pre-domesticated life, as well as the wild animals coming closer and closer," Alicia remarked one day.

"Yeah. It seems like yesterday that the monkeys started to come into the city."

"I would have to look back to what we were doing when we first spotted one in a tree not far from here. Now we hear the Howler Monkeys all the time."

"It isn't hard to imagine what this whole area was like before people settled and changed the land so much" David mused.

"I wonder what this area will look like 50 years from now."

"Likely what it looked like 50 years before the area was settled. Don't you agree?"

And, she did.

Actually, having looked back at the calendar, they decided it really hadn't been all that long after 'the incident' when they saw their first wild monkey in the city. It was a process of more and more wild sounds that could be heard in the early morning, growling and calling from the trees in a nearby park. For a time, several years later, David and Alicia had to keep their large picture window closed and partially screened to keep monkeys from coming in the house, stealing food and creating chaos. After a while, the monkeys seemed to conclude that they weren't welcome and, while they could still be seen and heard in the neighborhood, they generally left the couple alone.

Early on, they decided to try to keep up the general neighborhood in which they lived. They couldn't perform all of the work that the city had offered in the area of maintenance and cleaning, but they staked out an area that they decided would be their responsibility. Otherwise the work would be too overwhelming and take precious time from daily tasks related to eating and maintenance.

David regularly mowed their lawn and that of their neighbors, at first using a gasoline powered mower he found in a neighboring garage, but later turning to the use of a scythe which he obtained at the *MegaBodega*. In addition, he cut the curb lots along their street for several houses on either side and across the street along the ravine that overlooked the river below.

He also tried to keep a nearby square-block park mowed, but found that he could only do so occasionally because of the territory involved. However, he did cut a piece of land down the block and across the street where he and Alicia often sat to enjoy the late afternoon or an early morning.

As sewers became plugged and water backed up after heavy rain storms, David tried to regularly keep theirs clean and those on surrounding streets where runoff could flood their yard or garage. He occasionally trimmed off the various plants and trees that were growing up from cracks in the roads and sidewalks. If nothing else, that made getting places in the golf carts much easier.

But all of this was totally impossible in places they no longer went frequently, and even the way to *MegaBodega* was growing wilder by the day. Seldom did they leave to go anywhere these days without the machete, something that every Costa Brava household had, to clear the way if necessary. Some things were getting easier and some were getting harder with time.

In the early years he accumulated as many duplicate items of appliances and equipment as he could. In his garage or that of the neighboring houses, he had warehoused dozens of microwaves, lawn mowers, generators, refrigerators, stoves and CD players. And, the parking lot at the nearby mall was somewhat filled by the various cars and trucks that he had "borrowed" in the first year. Eventually, there were at least two dozen solar-powered golf carts that became their main source of transportation in the later years.

This was all very good, though some things did not do well stored in the moist climate and ultimately needed to be discarded.

Alicia's daily routine was a little more limited geographically, but nevertheless equally as demanding and crucial to their survival. After all, it was her role to not only cook, but also to help acquire food, prepare it for storage, protect it from mold, mildew and invading wildlife and to improvise where some things were unavailable.

She had long enjoyed cooking and had compiled numerous cookbooks and a large collection of recipes from around the world, reflecting the cuisine of the various countries where they had lived. She continued to use those for a while until the exotic spices ran out and several items weren't available. Soon, her task was to just keep food on the table and cook with the produce from their garden, or what survived years of storage. Fortunately, David had never been a picky eater and would consume just about anything she prepared, making the task much easier for her.

Her activities weren't tied to the kitchen or even to their apartment however. Often she joined him in one of the gardens to weed, plant and harvest. She almost always went with him when he went "shopping" at the *MegaBodega* or any of the other stores to which he had obtained access. There were things that she wanted and needed, and he never had been a good shopper. Even a shopping list was not always useful, in that he was more than likely to freelance, picking up odd things that he saw or thought he wanted while "forgetting" several items on the list.

And with time there were fewer and fewer items available at *MegaBodega*, so why go? Going there was also a little disgusting with mold and mildew, rot and slimy floors as well as an abundance of mice and roaches living off the things they had not taken in the first years. It was depressing. The buildings, too, were not immune from vines, roof leaks and crumbing walls…all of which damaged the "merchandise".

In the case that David went alone, the conversation was kind of like this, "Did you find the measuring spoons and any cinnamon I asked for?"

"You didn't ask for measuring spoons, did you?"

"Well, yes I did? If you didn't get the things on the list, I am afraid to ask what you did find," she would say.

"I got the cinnamon," he chirped, proud of himself. "And I found the neatest thing."….and he would give her a list of his "treasures", none of which were of value to her. With a sigh she decided if she wanted something, she would have to go along rather than trust David alone. And most of the time she did just that, despite her disgust over the deterioration she would see. Also, she preferred not to be separated too far or long from David.

Alone the same line, "I remember the day when the lawnmowers and shovels were nice and shiny. They are beginning to rust and are covered with ash from the eruption. I wonder if they will even work if I did try to start them." David muttered as they rummaged through the stores.

"Yes, the towels and sheets and other linens are all smelling musty, not that we need anymore. We got what we needed long ago. I hate that smell" Alicia exclaimed with a note of disgust and sadness in her voice.

"I guess it is more important than ever to take care of what we already have. That by itself is such a tiring task with all of the rain and humidity in the tropics, isn't it?"

Sometimes I just get weary and wonder if we should have just given up long ago" she said, her voice sounding a bit discouraged.

"Alicia, we have worked so hard to survive. We are not going to give up or get discouraged now. Or, at least I'm not, and I don't want you to either. We need each other too much."

The best she could do was respond with a weak, "I won't. I'm just in a funk some days. And this is one of those days."

Days stretched into years, and though they tried to keep track of time, it seemed to all blend together. Each year they had to make up a new calendar, if they happened to forget to mark it off the day homemade version, they wondered how accurate they were.

"Why are we bothering with a calendar?" Alicia asked one day.

"Because all humans need some semblance of order…the ancient peoples marked the seasons, using the sun and moon. I guess we are no different in some ways. Even people in prison keep track of the days they will be there, don't they?"

"Yes, but it seems silly to me. Who will ever see it? But we will keep doing it", she added in a *roll-your-eyes* voice.

To add a bit of levity to the conversation, David added, "Maybe we are doing it for the little green men who will invade Earth someday." This produced a smile and chuckle from both of them.

Alicia enjoyed reading, and would go to one of the embassy or English-school libraries to obtain material. Though the books also were beginning to mold and smell musty, she reminded David how much she hated that smell when he or she brought in the books.

In whatever "spare" time she had she also picked up painting as a hobby, clearing out from an art store at the mall, the materials she wanted. She started by developing several versions of the view from their panoramic front window, but later moved to depicting flowers, trees and tropical plants that were now prolific all around the neighborhood as the environment went more and more wild. Some of her creations adorned their walls after a period of time.

Then there were the discussions: the theological ones, the ones that explored, challenged, discouraged, gave hope and left many questions unanswered at best.

They had both grown up in Christian homes and were regular church-goers, especially in English-language, multinational congregations that dotted the globe in major international cities.

Their faith had, indeed, been challenged by what happened that took humanity, but they had never reached an understanding of why it occurred and why they survived. Why *did* it happen? They sought for a divine explanation, but never quite found one. Yet they often felt a sense of His purpose for what happened.

If anything, they raised more questions than it answered. Didn't God promise Noah that He would never destroy the earth again? Isn't this the promise of the rainbow? The promise from God gave them some *hope* that they weren't, in fact, the last people on earth. It was that hope that explained many of their early activities, making attempts to reach any other survivors of the incident by battery-powered ham radio or using other technology. They built a fire for anyone looking for them as survivors. Though finally, they resigned themselves to their solitude.

They regularly scanned the hills and city for any signs of survivors. They even considered, but quickly dismissed, the idea of making a difficult overland or possible sea voyage back to the United States, but soon accepted that futility. Beside, these two really did feel like the city was their true home, and that influenced their decision to stay put.

What got old after a while was the lack of contact with other people. This subject came up so frequently that they sounded like a broken record. They had always been quite sociable, mixing both in the local society, and, particularly, in the ex-pat community into which they fit perfectly. There had always been a dinner to attend, a service at the local international English-language church, a concert to fill the evening or a party to celebrate someone's arrival or departure. While they were very close and got along well, they still longed for the wider human contact that they had experienced all of their lives.

But, given the circumstances and challenges that confronted them, they did very well. On some occasions they felt they had too much time to be together and to think about the changing ways they experienced. Overall, though, they were upbeat and confident.

"Not bad," David mused one evening to Alicia as they stared at the view outside their window. "For pampered urban people, we are surviving quite well in this pre-industrial society in which we are living, don't you think?" And Alicia agreed, adding, "So far."

David was always the one that moved more confidently into most situations, while Alicia experienced a little more skepticism. That was reflected even in her last words, "so far," which indicated that she might not be as confident, or that she thought or feared that something could change. She was always ready to brace herself a bit against eventualities.

They still reflected on what killed everyone around them. After a while they stopped talking about it so much. They just referred to it as *that day* or *the incident*. "We will likely go to our graves without ever knowing," Alicia observed one day. "I guess we have been too busy just surviving to think much. We used to contemplate a lot, at least I did."

David agreed in a somewhat sober voice.

Chapter 14

David and Alicia were spending a quiet late afternoon sitting on the couch in front of their expansive picture window. This was what they called their "day of rest". After the labor of the week, reading and cross-stitching a scene from her huge stock she had brought from the U.S. many years ago, was relaxing. Except for some jobs, like feeding the chickens or cows that absolutely needed to be done, it was a relaxed time.

It always reminded Alicia of the day she decided to take Wednesday off to replace Saturdays at the university when she had classes to teach. So she announced to the other teachers and everyone else, "Don't call me unless you are sick or the building is on fire." She included David in that announcement. It gave her a peaceful day to wind down a bit from her hectic schedule. Sometimes she slept, and at other times she never got out of her PJs until just before David would be home at the end of his work day.

Now, without a daily newspaper or live TV or radio, the couple's entertainment was mostly books and CDs, though they occasionally watched a video when they had generated enough electricity.

This day, David was reading a novel about the early British immigrants to Chile and Alicia had been busying herself by yet another cross stitch.

"David."

No response.

"David," she repeated. "I think we ought to take a vacation. A change of scenery would be wonderful, don't you think?"

David chuckled as he kept his nose in the book. "Sure Hon, I think I have a few unused frequent flier miles. Maybe we could hop up to Miami for the weekend. Or, how about flying over to the beach at San Andres? That sounds great, doesn't it?"

"David," Alicia spit out. "I'm serious; I need to get away from all of this…this craziness and routine. I think that a week at the beach would be great. We don't have anything keeping us here that we could not go away for at least a week. The cats died a while back, and, with good planning, the gardens could take care of themselves, so to speak. What do you think, seriously? Couldn't we put extra food on the ground for the chickens? They could survive on that, couldn't they? The cows forage anyway and are dry right now", she added. She had David's attention now.

There was still silence until David heard her sniffle. He could tell she was now aggravated by his reaction. Quickly he put down his book and moved over toward her, but she stopped him with her arm. Tears were beginning to gather in her eyes. His flippant attitude frustrated her.

"Hon, I'm sorry. I didn't realize that you were so serious. And, my first reaction was, and really still is, that you've got to be kidding. How on the good earth are we supposed to take a vacation when we are basically trapped here in…in paradise?"

"I don't know," she said. "I know that going anywhere like we used to is impossible, but there must be something that we can do here just to get away for a while."

"Every day we look at the same things, do the same things, and work all day until we are worn out. Sure, we make certain that Sunday is different—we go to the church building, even in its decaying shape, and pray for a while, we read here at home, we listen to music, we walk to the park, but week in and week out we do the same thing and like you say, we are trapped in this life. I just need to get away, to do something completely different. I am so weary at times with the whole situation!"

The two sat in silence while they considered what she had said.

"I agree with what you are saying about the same routine day in and day out. OK, Hon," David slowly ventured. "I hear you, and I actually wouldn't mind getting away myself. So, rather than say that it is impossible, let's consider the possibilities."

"Given that we can't fly anywhere or take a cruise and that going outside of Costa Brava, let alone a long distance within the country, is just about impossible, what are some of the possibilities that you would like?"

Alicia thought for a while. "A long weekend at a full-service resort would be the idea" she added with a snicker. But, that being out of the question…David, would it be possible, I mean, do you think that we just might be able to go to the beach for a few days or a week or so? We don't know if the roads are still passable after the volcano exploded, or if they are too overgrown, but could we try that? I admit it would take lots of planning…food, and equipment if there were no facilities in good enough shape to stay."

"Wow. I don't know. I would have to think about it for a while. It sure would take a lot of planning" he added in a long drawn out voice.

Tropical beaches had become one of the couple's favorite vacation destinations over the years. During a stint in Thailand they had indulged themselves with regular trips to that country's fabled beaches to the south of Bangkok. In Spain they had frequented the Mediterranean beaches on the country's southern coast. And, here in Costa Brava they had absolutely fallen in love with Playa Langosta, a wild stretch of palm-lined beach on the Atlantic coast that fulfilled anyone's stereotype of a tropical playground.

There, the jungle came to the edge of the sand while monkeys of several varieties played in the nearby trees. Sloths, raccoons and a variety of sea birds were visible on any given day. And, except for the Holy Week and Christmas week-long holidays, the beach had been mostly deserted most weekdays. Not that this would be a problem under present circumstances. But, it was to there that they fled for regular vacations and to which Alicia had set her heart now.

But, how many years had it been since they lounged on the awesome beaches under the palms? Had swum in the emerald water of the coast of Costa

Brava? Enjoyed the hippy, relaxed way of beach village life? That did sound wonderful, but...

"Gosh. I dunno, Hon," David sort-of mumbled as he continued to think out loud. "It's a long way now with a solar-powered golf cart as transportation, and, as you mentioned, who knows what the condition of the roads will be. With earthquakes, landslides, floods, washed-out bridges and who knows what else that has occurred over the past years or so, I can't imagine what we will find."

"So, you are saying it's impossible?" Alicia snapped, losing patience with David who normally would take on any challenge. She was not used to the hesitancy that he was demonstrating.

"No, not impossible, but it will be a lot of work. We will have to go prepared for a long, slow trip, a difficult trip, and maybe an impossible trip." was David's pensive reply.

"Well, what do you think? Still seem impossible? Would you give consideration at least?" Alicia realized that David was getting on board with the idea and just might be fully behind it if she would give him some time to mull it over.

David responded slowly. "Again, I think....I think that if we plan correctly and solve as many of the foreseen problems, just like we did when *the incident* happened, we can do it."

She knew that it would not be long before he would be like a bat out of a cave, moving in all directions to put the plan together. And when he was done, all would be in order and ready...all eventualities considered based on their present knowledge. The trip would all be executed and managed the best it could be under their present circumstances.

Overjoyed, and now excited, that David would at least consider it, Alicia slid over next to him and took his hand. "Thank you. I appreciate it. I really need a trip…a get-away."

Chapter 15

It had been a long time since they had taken a real break from the routine. There was always work, work, and more work, particularly initially after *the event*, with always some down time scheduled in to keep up their spirits. All along they had tried to balance their life between the overwhelming responsibilities and the need for rest, relaxation, renewal and a break from the daily routine.

Once their mere survival depended solely on the couple, long trips were out of the question as well as physically impossible. With no air travel or any other type of public transportation, they felt that any getting away had to be done on a local basis. And it could only happen when they felt that they had the time.

Initially, gardening, hunting, gathering up goods, improvising their living conditions, generating power and the myriad of things that they had to do just to survive took all of their energy. And, after petroleum-powered transportation became impossible, a long trip also seemed impossible.

Eliminating their use of their vehicles and gasoline they had amassed took a physical toll on them. It meant more major changes as well carting replacements for the heavier items that might wear out or disintegrate. Prior to giving up the vehicles and parking them at the mall, they checked and rechecked for anything of value to them left in any store that they had "looted". And from that monumental final day, and somewhat emotional point in their new life, they relied on slower solar-powered golf carts to get them around.

They transferred their place of worship to a small modern Roman Catholic chapel which they had maintained near their house so they could walk or ride a short distance. It was just easier to get to than the international church they had once attended.

For a time they also semi-maintained two additional houses to which they could go for a change of scenery and to get away. The first: that of the Von Boem's, only about seven blocks from their apartment. They chose this location because they were very familiar with the house. They also saw it as an alternative to their own apartment should it be damaged by fire or an earthquake or if an infirmity or age made it necessary for them to live on one floor rather than have to climb to their third-floor apartment.

Quite often on Sunday they would go there after "church" to spend time cleaning the weeks' worth of dust, taking care of the lawn, working in the garden, checking out the wonderful tropical fruits that still grew on the property and then cooking out and just relaxing. Often they would spend a night or two there carrying with them whatever linens they needed so they did not have to do laundry in two places. They saw it as a weekend away, and it was always refreshing.

Their other retreat was a home high in the hills over San Juan which belonged to their friends, the Griffiths. John, a British citizen, had lived in Costa Brava for nearly twenty-five years. He had grown up in the British colony in Santiago, Chile, had met his wife Clare, a U.S. citizen in college in England and operated an import-export business while Clare taught at one of the international schools.

This was the place where Alicia and David would retreat to for a day-trip of hiking or just relaxing on the veranda of the Griffiths spacious home with a panoramic view of the mountains and the valley spread out before them. The property also contained a number of unusual fruit trees as well as berry bushes which they harvested every time they went.

Both places had amenities and food supplies that lasted for a while before they had to start taking their own. After a while that location became overrun with vegetation and was difficult maintain. Also, it had always been just a bit too far, even with the vehicles.

In recent years they did not go often and, in fact, it had been just over a year since they made the trip up the mountain. While only an hour away by automobile, via a solar-powered golf cart, the long haul up the steep mountain with deteriorating roads and over growth could take up to three hours.

And then, while at John and Clare's house, the first part of the day had to be spent cutting the lawn and often making urgent repairs to the house. After a while, it seemed that the work keeping up the facility far outweighed the needed rest, change of location and recreation. So, in spite of the respite, their trips up the mountain would become non-existent.

Planning a trip to the beach in a car, normally a two to three-hour trip depending on the slow moving trucks carting goods back and forth over the mountains, seemed almost impossible now with slow golf carts. But, after agreeing to give it a try, they charged forward with their plans as they had always done in their lives.

And, they still needed to keep up the apartment and gardens until the day they left so they would not come back and find they had no food.

"Hon, we need to consider what we could run into and try to take enough stuff to get us around any problem points." David said the next day as they were beginning to iron out details for the trip.

"Like what?" Alicia inquired.

"Well, the most difficult part will be finding the road open all the way there. You know, landslides, earthquakes and floods as well as just plain deterioration and washouts on Costa Brava's notoriously bad roads will be a challenge. I've been thinking—do you remember the old way over to the beach?"

"The road around the other side of Mt. Tronodor?" Alicia asked.

"Right," David replied. "The more direct road goes through rougher territory and was always subject to landslides—it would be closed three or four times a year, sometimes for several days."

"Yes, I remember well! Yet you hardly ever heard about the old road being closed."

"Right," David replied. "It was always two or three hours longer but there were fewer cuts through hillsides and the mountains weren't right up against the highway. I think we would have a better chance of getting through that way."

"Ok, how long do you think it would take to get to Playa Langosta Beach the old way?"

David thought a bit. The old road used to take about five or six hours at an average speed of thirty-five miles an hour. The golf carts can go about fifteen to twenty miles an hour. So, figuring that at just over half of the speed of a car on Costa Brava highways, the elapsed driving time would be around twelve to fifteen hours.

"I think that we should figure at least two days, maybe three, to get there and two or three to get back assuming no major blockages from landslides and no bridges washed out," David announced.

"David, that's not too bad. But, what happens if we run into the slides or a missing bridge."

"Well, the worst thing is that we would have to abort the trip short of the beach, or, if the missing bridge is along the coast, consider another beach rather than going to Playa Langosta," David explained. "The other things we need to consider are the range of the batteries and the need to stop to change or charge the extra batteries we take with us, the time we will need to clear the road from fallen trees and rocks, maneuver around other blockages including landslides and so forth. But, I think it is doable."

Alicia breathed a sigh of relief. "It seems overwhelming. What have I talked you into?" She smiled and paused.

"Well, we go as far as we can, and if it doesn't work we turn around. You know, David, we have overcome so many obstacles during these past years, and we have done things that neither of us had any experience with or knowledge about, but we have done them. If we can survive this far, certainly we can get to the beach for a week."

"I agree. Now, the challenge for you is how we will handle two weeks of food without any storage or any of our gardens here."

"Piece of cake," she replied, chuckling when she realized what she had said. "You know that I have canned much of what you produced that we don't eat right away. Along the way we'll find fruit—at least bananas and papayas and probably mangos and other fruit. We'll start out with water from our storage barrels and since the coast gets some rain even in dry season we'll be able to catch some drips off of leaves. And, who knows, maybe you can catch a monkey or other wild animals to eat while we are there."

David nodded his head in agreement. He never worried about food when Alicia was around, nor a good, balanced diet. She was very careful about that.

He had decided that they would each drive a separate cart in case one broke down and to provide more carrying space for what they needed to take along. Finally, he decided to modify one of the six-passenger golf carts that he had commandeered from a local golf course. He knew that the slower, longer cart might slow down their trip, maybe making their one-way trip from 2 days to three, but it would help to carry the equipment including extra batteries to power the carts.

Regular work in the garden and house continued to be done, but preparations for the trip consumed several hours each day. Modifying the already-solar-powered carts to carry additional panels, he attached them to extra batteries that they were carrying so that they could charge as they traveled. In each cart he measured out space for camping equipment and the storage of food and clothing, though the latter was the least of their worries at the beach where they would be in swimsuits much of the time.

The couple packed and repacked the carts several times to make sure they were using the space most efficiently. But, it was tight. In addition to the goods needed for living, David considered equipment that they might need; shovels and rakes to work their way around landslides and bad patches of road, several lengths of wood that might be used to cross a stream where a bridge had washed out, a hammer, several saws, ropes, a first-aid kit, extra sun glasses and two firearms, just in case.

With all of the preparation, one or the other of them would question if it was all worthwhile. However, once David was on board with the idea of a beach trip, it was if nothing would stop him, and Alicia was the one who would wonder most about the sanity of such a trip.

Despite, they both pressed forward and in only two weeks they were prepared to set off.

"David, thanks so much," Alicia said as she kissed him after dinner the night before departure. "Even if we don't get much past the city, as least you were willing to try. I appreciate that."

Chapter 16

Several hours into the first day of the trip, if David had thought about Alicia's words much, he might have wondered if she knew how prophetic her thoughts in the past might be. The day had been long, alternatively hot and wet, and very tiring. The couple knew that the roads through the city would be fairly open even though scattered with bones of long-ago decomposed bodies of people who had dropped dead on that fateful day. They had traveled those streets frequently in the car, stopping originally to pull a few people to the side of the road so they could pass by. But, once they left the small town of León, it became obvious that the lack of any kind of traffic had taken its toll. Trees lay across the two lanes, one of them impassable without an hour of difficult work sawing logs and casting them aside. Some of them were so heavy it took concerted effort to roll them to the side to allow enough space to pass.

The country's infamous potholes had become more prolific, at times certainly large enough to swallow one of the carts let alone a small compact car. Each time they were able to pass by, but each encounter with an obstacle slowed down the progress putting them further behind.

Like clockwork, a noon-time shower blew over them off the volcano leaving them damp and shivering despite the tropical heat. Later, a pack of dogs charged the vehicles forcing David to shoot several times in the air to scare them off.

Despite several years of heavy rainstorms all of the bridges in the central valley seemed to have weathered the climate, though at one point they had to get off and test an old structure before rolling across. They both wondered, with the shoddy construction of Costa Brava, if any of them would collapse under the weight of their loaded carts. *Save where you can on the finances, so you can line your pocket* was sometimes the mentality of construction in this beautiful country.

At one such crossing, the memory of a high bridge they encountered over a decade ago came to mind. It seems that the work crew hadn't followed the engineering directions closely enough. Construction started at either end with the goal of meeting in the middle, but that did not quite happen. The funny jog of the lanes had always amused and worried them and made them wonder, just a bit, about the sturdiness of any span they crossed in the country.

Worries about bridges included another crossing over a deep and fairly wide canyon they drove over years ago before *the incident*. How would it fare in one of the frequent earthquakes? Their previous experience of getting stopped on another bridge because of a light at one end had caused them concern, particularly as a truck would rumble by in the opposite lane, shaking the structure. Would the bridge hold up and if not would the couple survive a hundred foot drop? It sent chills through them just thinking about it. The answer was not in their favor,

By five p.m. they had ascended the mountain into the cooler and damper air. The climb up the steep road had also slowed their progress—the battery-powered carts didn't have the pull to go faster, especially with the heavy loads. Soon, they found that two sets of batteries were very low on power, though they had set the first one to recharging around one p.m.

Coming upon a small mountain town, the couple decided that they had pushed on enough for the first day. Finding a hotel in the town's center, they went from room to room seeking the cleanest, least cockroach overrun, most comfortable setting to spend the night. Fortunately for them, most Latin American hotels had not installed the electronic entry cards preferred by the more upscale places, so grabbing a set of keys from the desk they were able to move quickly through the hotel searching.

Soon, they found a room that had not been inhabited the night that all human life ceased, so they were able to do a quick sweeping out of the cobwebs, ants as well as the leaves that had blown in. After adding their own clean sheets and a light blanket over the musty, still-made bed, they felt they could be comfortable enough to sleep on it. Despite the warm days, they knew to expect cold nights. They took out their own towels, though showers no longer had running water, and they would cart a little water from a nearby stream coming off the mountains to wash up. They soon found themselves comfortably settled.

"Not bad, right?" David asked as they relaxed before going to sleep. "I wasn't sure how fast we might move but we got almost as far as I expected, I guess."

"It was fine," Alicia replied. "I didn't know what to expect either, but I guess I thought that we would speed along the highway like we always did. I should have known better. But, I'm satisfied. And, it's kind of nice to move up the mountain highway slower—you don't have to watch for other traffic or trucks going too fast in your lane and you can enjoy the scenery. I really enjoyed today, David. Thanks."

David nodded. It had been a beautiful day, and it was so good to be in the countryside again after so long confined to the city, particularly in its present state. They had reminisced about their many previous trips on the mountainous roads, rolling through small towns, stopping for fresh fruit, visiting souvenir shops and craft exhibits by local artisans on the way.

It was certainly different now with shops barely showing their wares through their lush green coverings of thick vines. The fruit trees were still offering their bounty, but rather than children hoping to lure customers in by holding up bags full of *avacates, mandarinas, Mamon Chinos* or bananas, David or Alicia had to pick their own or glean what had fallen from the trees if they could not reach them. Some took more tramping through vegetation while worrying about possibly encountering a snake or other form of wildlife—more than they cared to do. Still there was plenty of delectable food available that had not been overgrown by vines.

The towns were recognizable because many consisted of familiar cement buildings and streets with trees planted years ago along the roads. These had grown to enormous heights, cracking the cheap quality cement of the sidewalks. Others had fallen on buildings, smashing them to bits.

But, the ever-extending jungle had taken over the outskirts creeping in all directions unrestrained. These towns also looked frozen in time with no activity and lots of skeletons lying on the streets just as they were when *the event* hit. Perhaps they had said goodbye to family that morning, like any day, fully expecting to return to them after work. Others appeared to be children with their dark blue pants or skirts and white shirts and necktie or blouses now draped over their small bones. No doubt they were on their way to their 7 a.m. to 1 p.m. class session. The skeletons came in all sizes.

Having seen just about everything in the city, nothing could totally shock David and Alicia, but what it did was stir within them again the question as to why they had survived and others did not. What could it have been to cause such a catastrophe? How many times had they discussed this? One hundred times? Perhaps.

But, passing through several settlements they still had been struck by how empty these once active vibrant towns seemed; no sign of human life anywhere, just all the skeletons from humans and dogs, long dead, scattering the road or on front stoops. The frequent hitch-hikers were gone as were those young couples heading out together along the road holding hands. About the only life that was familiar were the occasional wild dogs, most of which kept their distance and looked with what seemed to be curiosity at these strange creatures passing through their territory.

In one town, the couple took a bit of time once to peruse the contents of a few of the stores along the way to see if there were any products of use to them. But that was a fruitless task, with their finding little that had not deteriorated beyond use or value. The wildlife--rats and roaches mostly had made the buildings that had once contained good food into nasty, repulsive, infested, undesirable locations.

At other times they would take quick breaks, stopping in the road. Why pull over when there was no traffic? Or they paused in a town and got out a snack, giving their imagination time to wonder what life would have been like in that village or on that stretch of road.

They peered into homes and schools that were not too badly overgrown and saw a scene frozen in time, exactly as it was. Though they thought they had seen it all and gotten used to such things, it still stirred thoughts, emotions and memories.

For periods of time they would roll along in single file each with their own thoughts, watching for potholes or obstacles that could disable one or the other of their golf carts and sabotage the trip and their desire to get to the beach.

At one point early in their trip when the road was wide enough to ride side by side in their individual carts, David remarked that the roads seemed to be narrower than he remembered. Alicia agreed quietly, then, broke into a soft laugh. "David, of course they seem narrower. There is much more overgrowth along the side and it's creeping onto the right of way! Naturally, it makes the highway look narrow."

All along the way they each made observations about the things they remembered and the beauty they had missed whizzing by in a vehicle run with gasoline.

Knowing it was not wise to travel after dark because of the danger of breaking down or the possibility of damage to the carts by falling into a pothole, they agreed each day to stop early for the night. Dawn would come as early as 5:30 a.m. in Costa Brava, giving them lots more daylight tomorrow.

Another reason to call it quits for the day was that wild animals and reptiles were plentiful. So as soon as the sun was at a certain point, they decided they should stop in the next village and see if they could find a place they could use for a safe shelter for the night.

It turned out to be a more difficult task than they expected. Everything had deteriorated and what might have been a perfectly nice place in the past was not exactly inviting anymore. They might have to choose between snakes on the first floor or roaches on the second. After a very short discussion, they both agreed on the second floor if available, neither enthusiastic about a snake crawling across them to get to its destination. They also realized they would have to ignore some things that were the result of neglect: mold, dust, musty smell, all of which were eliminated in their apartment in the city because Alicia constantly worked to keep their home pleasant.

The best way to eliminate these un-pleasantries was to keep the windows wide open, which they did.

Out of nowhere Alicia remarked, "Gosh it was nice having a maid. I could leave a load of dishes in the sink, floors that needed to be cleaned and come back to a spic and span apartment. How I miss that!"

"Yes. It left you more time to do other things," was his muted response.

There was no point mulling too much over Alicia's point, so having found a passable place to stay, they whipped it into the best level or standard they could by using their small broom, as well as a few rags they had brought and water from a nearby stream of water.

It was relaxing for both of them to think back over the beautiful birds, flowers and other vegetation that could be seen only at the various altitudes through which they had traveled. What a rejuvenating day it had been for each of them.

With dark coming at 6:30 or 7:00, they ate a small meal that Alicia had prepared. Then, wanting to save battery light, they went to sleep hoping to get an early start.

David was up at daybreak knowing that a day in Costa Brava was about 12 hours of daylight and there was much to do and miles to go. His day began checking the vehicles and making sure that everything was ready to go. Two of the three sets of batteries for each vehicle were at full charge and he expected that the third set would recharge from the solar panels during the first part of the day, f there was enough sunlight in the rain forest, now thicker than it was back when things were normal. Checking the wheels he found that everything was in order and all of the supplies so carefully packed were secure. *"So far so good."* he thought.

He and Alicia cleaned up the room, in case they wanted to stay at the same place on the way back, repacked their clothes and supplies, ate a bit of cold food Alicia had prepared and were underway by six-thirty a.m. with the usual jungle noises as their backdrop. David fully expected this day to be the slowest in terms of speed in that they needed to crest the mountain range that ran along the entire east side of San Juan and then move down into the intervening valleys before dropping off into the tropical coastal lowlands. His main worry was that there might be some blockage because of landslides through the mountainous terrain.

And, indeed, the day went much as expected with challenges that took their energy and some ingenuity as the road had mud filled craters as well as major washouts.

They stopped early for lunch along a river where while David changed the batteries on the golf-carts, Alicia used a solar heater that David had designed to heat some food. They snacked on fruit from trees that they had found along the road. Late in the day they passed about forty miles south of the Shifrin Volcano, another less-active mountain not visible from the city. Here, the road showed even more deterioration as small streams and some flooding rivers had worn away the pavement leaving the way rocky and full of potholes.

By just before nightfall they had reached the last town before the road descended to the tropical plain below. A little behind their original schedule, they stopped early but again found all of the buildings in very bad shape, this time because of volcano-caused earthquakes.

Unable to find a hotel, they decided to pitch their tent near what was once a large grove of papaya trees still bearing fruit. After some chopping with the machete, David was able to clear enough space and pitch the pup tent on a ground cloth for protection against protruding stalks and debris. They settled in for the evening and night. They reviewed the day, labeling it another good experience with not too many insurmountable challenges.

"Our preparation has paid off. So far there isn't anything that we have needed that we did not have or couldn't scrounge for," David reflected.

"Yes, and I am glad I put the time into preparing a couple of meals that I did not have to heat up last night and tonight when I am tired. And so far the ice that I was able to make has held up." Alicia remarked.

"The meals have been good." David remarked, always ready to compliment her on her culinary skills and the finished products.

"Most of the fresh stuff I could bring will be used up very soon, as well as the ice, so it may be things I have canned after tomorrow."

"We will be just fine," he assured her. "You won't hear me complaining."

"No, you never do. I think I could serve you a terrible meal and you would find something nice to say about it," she said with a chuckle.

Little did they know, with this light banter, what was ahead of them. It was along the coast that their trip almost ended unexpectedly.

Chapter 17

The next day found them making much better time, despite a couple of pauses again to clear small trees and branches. They descended from the *cordillera* to the hot, muggy plain below. While the heat was more intense than what they were used to in the central valley, the road was much more level and they were able to move along with greater speed even though the highway was laced with the usual potholes. The bridges seemed more treacherous and shaky, at times causing them to hold their breath, hoping they would hold up.

The highlight of the trip from San Juan to Playa Langosta was the coastal road that wound along the curving coastline from Puerto Cabezas, the country's largest port. The beach along the road was littered with driftwood and a little trash that had not yet disintegrated through the years. However, there was no new debris since there were no people to create it.

Tall palm trees lined the road just a hundred yards or so from the crashing waves. But the highlight of that ride was their first view of the emerald green waters, darkened in spots by the shadows of the clouds, some of which were green on the bottom as they reflected the color of the sea.

The coastal view, after being in the higher elevations, always took the couple's breath away. And this time it was no different. They could not help but pull over under the shade of the palms and just take it in. As they looked Alicia could feel the tensions of the last few years and the trip down drain from her.

"Can you beat this?"

"It is almost more beautiful than I remember," was their exchange before they just stood there quiet, drinking it all in. Having jettisoned their shoes, they wiggled their toes in the sand and remarked on the color of the water. They rejoiced at the white foam created by waves breaking on the sugar white sand and then drifting out to sea before the next wave came.

Nothing had changed about the scene, and yet there was something that caused them to discuss what it might be.

"There are no ships. They used to be coming and going from the port," David commented.

"Ahh, yes," Alicia nodded. "But, where are they? It seems we would see them still anchored out at sea on their long chains they had to hold the anchor."

"I imagine they broke away in a storm and sank out at sea or maybe rusted enough to just sink in place when a hurricane came along," David commented.

"What a difference the absence of people and natural forces make on this earth," she mused.

Moving along the narrow bridges, now in various levels of deterioration, they spanned the various creeks and rivers that drew water off of the mountains and deposited it into the sea. In places, overgrown banana plantations spread inland, complete with their sagging overhead lines that had once carried the ripened stems to the processing plant where they were made ready to be shipped to places around the world.

There were still bananas growing, though they were hard to get to and in various stages of ripeness. Finally they found a spot where they were able to reach a few, some ripe for now and others to have later.

There were no transport trucks, of course, to get bananas from the tropical coast to San Juan, so the taste after years without them was like ambrosia. Both said nothing, but let out a long "Ummm" with the first bite. Not eating themselves sick on them took restraint after all these years. They agreed to limit themselves to one or, at the most, two per day.

Along the beach highway were a dozen or so once beautiful, but now dilapidated, resorts, as well as one or two environmental stations marked by clusters of overgrown houses in what had been small communities. They recalled fond memories of the old roadside markets and stands that sold coconut water.

On the beach side, the travelers could still catch glimpses of the blue-green ocean sparkling in the sun between the palm trees and other jungle growth. Those who were driving pre-*event* and willing to explore could have pulled off into one of the numerous sand paths that ran off toward the water and could have walked to the almost always empty, pristine beaches.

It was from one of those beaches that David and Alicia had hauled off a four-foot piece of driftwood shaped by the action of the waves more artistically fashioned than any human hand or mind could have comprehended. Even those many years later that driftwood still held a spot outside of their apartment door, a centerpiece for a small potted tropical flower garden that Alicia continued to maintain despite the need for more practical cultivations.

"You can hardly get a glimpse of the ocean now," David commented with a bit of sadness in his voice.

"Yeah, but one nice thing is that once we get to Langosta, the ocean will still be rolling in."

"Yes. How much can that have changed?" David continued.

"Well," Alicia responded stretching out the word. "It did before the last time that we were here, and might have again. Remember the earthquake that lifted the ocean floor three feet?"

"It cut off this whole area for how long? All I remember was once having to ford a stream in our old Trooper and barely getting through," added David.

"So all bets are off that the ocean will not have changed in this amount of time since we were last here," Alicia added with a note of skepticism in her voice. "Let's just hope for the best after this long trip. One way or another I think it will still be beautiful. If we only get this far, I will be happy."

And the conversation seemed to just fade off into their individual thoughts again as they rode on side by side, with only the hum of the solar powered carts.

After a while they became more and more anxious to just push through to their destination. Neither of them knew why but tension seemed to come out of nowhere. Maybe it was because the trip slowed considerably, testing their resolve and patience. They had made good time on the down-hill portion from the central *cordillera* and through the much flatter territory between the mountains and the coast. But, shortly after turning onto the coastal highway and the first stretch out of Puerto Cabezas, one obstacle after another blocked the path. The washed-out road made the going rough, and dozens, if not hundreds, of fallen trees played havoc with their schedule as well as their normally mellow dispositions.

Each of them had thoughts of doom that they did not express or explain.

After sawing their way through a few trees, each stop taking up to an hour or more, the couple finally decided that they needed to find another way around them.

"The beach! Why didn't I think of it earlier?" said David as more a statement than a question, slapping his head dramatically as he suddenly realized that he had not been thinking clearly about alternatives. "How stupid I am not to think of using the beach as our highway."

"It would be a much better route. You're right!" Alicia said, quickly coming on board with David's idea. "I was concentrating so much on clearing the road that I didn't even think about that possibility."

Making their way to the next old turn out, both hopped out of the carts and, using their machetes, cleared the path down to the broad, sandy expanse. And there it was again, the ocean, as beautiful as ever. Emerald green with white billowy clouds in the sky building for the day's rainy period that was certain to come. It was so beautiful that they were again speechless.

Again David, in a quiet voice, broke the spell. "We had better go if we are going to finish this trip today."

"Yes. But isn't it beautiful? I can hardly get enough of it," Alicia added dreamily, not expecting a response.

Getting the carts through the soft sand took some time and a lot of pushing, but on reaching the harder beach moistened by the tide, they found themselves making slow but regular progress.

At the first stream crossing they tested the water's depth enjoying the cool water washing over their feet and legs. And they decided that the vehicles could make it across with little trouble. Indeed, the next several streams afforded an easy crossing, and they found themselves making fairly good time toward their destination. But that was not to last.

They arrived at the Rio Blanco, a river of water that was much wider and faster compared to the meandering streams they had forded earlier. To test the depth, David waded out into the water and found that it quickly came up to his chest. He could tell his feet were losing traction and contact with the river bottom, spelling trouble. His heart began pounding with fear. It would not have been the first time to come close to losing his life by being swept out to sea at a beach with a steep incline and crashing waves. It happened once along the Pacific coast, and the thought of something similar here scared him beyond words.

This was too close for comfort. He went down deeper into the water hoping to get some traction, and pushed off toward shore with all of his strength. Instead, he lost his footing and started moving ever so rapidly in the swift current toward the ocean.

Alicia let out a scream, knowing what was happening. David began to try to swim toward the bank, but to no avail. The harder he tried the worse the situation became. He was swiftly heading exactly where he did not want to go…towards the sea and deeper water.

Alicia, beginning to panic, yelled in her loudest voice, "Swim at cross angles to the current!" She repeated the same words and went as far as the jungle vegetation would allow in the same direction as David was moving. But she came to a place that would not allow her to go any further and she stopped, watching him move further from her.

She continued to scream, "David, move at a 90 degree angle! David, swim at right angles to the current!" She had no idea if he could hear her, but shear panic would not let her stop. Finally, she collapsed on the beach sobbing, with thoughts running rampant… *All she could think of what was what David was going through…drowning. And, she felt totally helpless and out of control. What would she do without him?*

Alicia was nauseated with each thought. She simply could not imagine life anymore.

She cried out to God to save him from this disaster. She had no idea how long she sat there, praying, crying and then thinking and praying and crying some more until she was weak. Despite her deep faith, her prayers each time were the same, *Lord give him strength to swim to safety. Help him remember the things we know about riptides. Help him to think clearly. Lord, help him survive.*

David had heard her pleas to move at a 90 degree angle, but was unable to get himself heading in the right direction. Finally, when he did, he continued to move along the bank like a crab moving sideways.

How many times had they read in the paper of someone who had drowned despite being a strong swimmer? Many times the person was overconfident in their swimming ability; sure they could get out of the riptide by swimming against the current. Always the article contained the advice to move at right angles and get out of the river of water to a calmer part of the ocean or river. That might be a great distance out and that is what always scared someone. But, reading about it and experiencing it were two different things. As hard as he tried he couldn't get himself to the side of the river. Compounding the problem was the fact that the tide was going out with each minute wave, dragging him ever faster.

Just beyond the mouth of the river, 1,000 feet or more from where he started, there was a sand bar that was shallower and the water slowed a little. He could feel the water slowing, but did not know why immediately. That was his only chance to keep himself from getting swept out to the deep ocean and drowning. Though he could still not touch bottom, the reduced current might help him he reasoned.

With a strength that could only come from a shot of adrenaline, he swam toward the edge of the river. He brushed by vegetation, but could not grab it, still moving too fast. Finally he grabbed a branch, but it was too fine and it snapped.

Coming closer to the bar he made an attempt to plant his feet. The first try was not successful, but ten feet away from that point, he felt firm ground and used the power in his legs to launch himself to shallow water.

Exhausted he crawled to a higher place on the bar. When he had caught his breath, he looked around, realizing for the first time how close he had come to the wide open sea.

The next observation was the density of the vegetation along the beach on the other side of the sand bar. Studying the situation while he rested, he decided that by crossing a much narrower and less swift stream also coming in at the same point, he could easily get to a walkable, though narrow, beach.

His goal was to get back to Alicia.

Dragging himself up onto the beach, he walked several yards away from the river in the direction they had come when stopped by the river. Not seeing any way to get to the part of the beach where Alicia would be without tramping through thick vegetation, he charged into what he hoped was not snake invested jungle. He was surprised at how wide that area was, as well as how thick the area was with tropical plants.

Being his usual determined self, he plodded on, making slow but steady progress. And, as he moved on he started to call to her, hoping she would hear and respond to give him a sense of direction and somehow be able to shorten the walk.

His calls went unanswered. Had he gone in the wrong direction? Was she OK? Had she gone in the water to try to rescue him and gotten caught up in the river and riptide? Was there too much ambient sound to deaden his calls to her?

Alicia sat for a long time trying to calm herself, thinking. *"Whatever made us not realize the danger and tie a rope to a tree and his waist?* And, how she regretted that the whole trip had been her idea.

Thinking that she heard a sound, her senses sharpened. Every time she thought she heard something, a sound of a crashing wave or the call of a bird or thunder in the distance would wake her to the reality that it was her imagination. There was no sound. She had not heard his voice, she was sure.

The thunder and the crashing waves increased, but then she was beginning to think it just might be his voice. Finally, she let out a loud answer, not knowing if she was just hoping she was hearing his voice or, indeed, was actually hearing him.

She moved slowly in the direction she thought she might have heard it and listened. Yes. It was David. Letting out a scream, she yelled over other sounds, "David!?" Then she listened. Silence. But in a short time another call came. Running in that direction, she screamed his name again and again. And, this time there was no mistake.

Guiding him to her like a lighthouse beacon, she waited. Slowly, he worked his way through the vegetation, not more than 25 feet from where she was standing.

Even though he was slightly bruised and bloodied from his walk through the jungle they grasped each in a tight embrace.

They stood like that for a long in spite of increasing thunder with an impending storm. They had been through one personal storm with this scare but were both so relieved to be able to hug the other that they did not let go.

Returning to the river bank where the carts were, they discussed the situation, sharing his near miss when he lost traction. They both chattered over each other with their thoughts and experiences. The situation had created such a tension, leaving them emotionally washed out. They debriefed for a while before moving on to other talk.

Decisions needed to be made.

During the conversation, they discussed what they and every person who had ever lived in Costa Brava knew, that if you were swept out with a riptide the likelihood of making it back to shore was little to none. Frequently there were reports of tourists who were never found. The whole idea of riptides hit too close to home when the teenage son of a close friend was on a school trip and never came home after swimming in the ocean near a river emptying into the ocean. Days of searching never produced a body.

"David, I am so sorry that I even proposed this whole trip." Then her next comment was, "I think we need to head back. I'm not sure that Playa Langosta is worth all this."

But David, with a take-command voice, answered Alecia with a resounding, "No. I don't agree with you at all. I think we need to move forward. We are so close."

"Yeah?" Alicia responded. "I thought I was going to lose you. I'm still tied in knots." Then added, "I would be be satisfied that we got this far."

The discussion went on with David standing his ground. Finally he presented her with a list of reasons and a solution to the problem of crossing this river.

Now, with a new respect for the river and its dangers, they pressed on.

Alicia reflected. "It's obviously too deep for the vehicles to make it across right now. The current will pick the carts up and take them and us out to sea."

David could hear the nervousness and doubt in her voice that they might not make it across. Her body language told it all as she seemed to sag like a rag doll as she stood with drooping shoulders and a long face.

"Never happen. We'll make it." David boasted in cheerful response to the lingering thought of being swept out to sea again by a riptide. "Though I have to admit I was a little unnerved there once or twice. Kinda like Daniel Boone," he added trying to add levity to a very serious situation."

"Daniel Boone? Whatever are you talking about? Is this going to be one of those corny jokes again? What does he have to do with this situation?"

"Well, you have heard the story of what old Daniel said once when he disappeared for a few days in the mountains of Kentucky, right?" David continues.

"No, I haven't," Alicia responded. "Tell me, mister historian, what did Old Daniel have to say?"

"Well, he said he was never lost in the woods, but he was mighty befuddled for a few days once."

Alicia groaned. She thought that she had heard all of David's sometimes good, often pretty bad jokes, but this was a new one. "It's not very funny in the light of the seriousness of the situation. I still don't see how it fits in with being dragged out to sea. And, where did you hear that for heaven's sake?"

"Oh, on *The Late Show* just the other day," he replied sarcastically with a smirk, knowing full well they no longer received broadcasts and hadn't for years."

"OK mister entertainer, thanks for the humor. But now, don't you think that we need to put our declining brainpower into figuring a way to get across this river?"

"Yup, of course," David responded. "Tell you what, I'm going to walk up to the bridge and see if we can get the vehicles up there and across that way. Let me scout out that possibility before we make any decisions. Sound like a plan?"

Alicia sadly watched him go off and later wished they had just moved the golf carts and she had gone with him. It was a little late to charge after him now.

Returning a half-hour later, much to Alicia's relief, David looked discouraged. Now it was his turn to look defeated. And, Alicia could never come up with any silly story like David could to break the tension.

"What's the matter? Is the bridge out?" Alicia asked.

"Yeah, you guessed it," he explained as he swung into the seat beside her in the cart and put his arm around her shoulder. "The whole bed of the bridge is gone and most of the pillars are washed away or crumbled. It looks like a mighty strong flash-flood came through here several years ago and washed the whole thing away."

"I scoured around to see if there were any steel beams or any sort of material that we could use to fashion some sort of a way to cross, but there was nothing, or what I found was way heavier than you and I together could move to provide support. Besides, it's even deeper there than here."

"Why is that?" she wondered.

"Well, here there is a bit of a sand bar that has built up from the wave action. See back there where the current seems a bit wider?" he said pointing back upstream.

"Yeah, I see it. Is that some backup from the sand bar?"

"I think so," David said pondering. "And, I'm thinking that the bar and or the pond may provide us with a possible opportunity."

"Yeah? What do you have in mind?"

"Well, first the tide is still up right now, so the water rushing out of the river is backed up a bit making it deeper even over the sand bar. But, when it goes down it may slow down the current or lower the water level, giving us a shot at getting across."

"I don't know," Alicia responded. "That sounds pretty risky even if it is lower. I'm not sure it would be safe. David, what if we cannot get back over this spot on the way back? We would be stuck here."

"We will cross that bridge when we get to it."

"David, that's not funny! I don't think I can stand any more humor. I don't want to be stuck here. I just want to enjoy the beach for a while. I am not in the mood for much more right now. I am really worn out. And I would think you are too."

"I am tired out. Sorry. I was just trying to add levity and solve our present problem."

"Now back to it being risky…I know what you are thinking," David added. "But, I have some ideas. First, let's have a snack so we have a little energy and a break for me to plan some more. We have to wait for the tide to go out anyway. This preparation will make use of the time it takes for the tide to cooperate.

Alicia obliged by producing a few things she had packed and a banana from the previous plantation they had passed.

Then they spent the next few hours making preparations for the crossing. David tied one of the life jackets on his wrist. If he had put it on as normally done, he might be assured of the current catching him and carrying him out to sea. On his wrist, he would have it if he needed it, but it would not add the buoyancy that would be dangerous if he lost his footing.

While he was doing that, he had Alicia tie a long length of rope securely around a palm tree and he fastened the other end around his waist. After they both checked the other's work, he cautiously made his way across the slightly lower river, stumbling several times but able to catch himself each time, he continued his crossing. Reaching the other side, he fastened the end he had put around his waist securely to another tree, making sure the rope was taut. And then he made his way back grasping the rope that was tied to the trees on both ends to make the trip easier and safer.

Using some huge clips and a short length of rope that he brought, he connected one of the carts to the guide rope. They put on their life vests, then, they were also hooked to the long rope they had stretched across the stream. That way, if the cart was washed out toward the sea, the individual would have an extra backup of being connected to the rope. He figured that either of them would be able to survive a catastrophic overturning or washing away of the vehicle. However, they hoped that his theory that the sandbar would be more exposed as the tide receded would keep all dangerous situations at bay.

They decided that once the tide was at its lowest point, Alicia would take the long, heavier cart across first, hoping the added weight of the larger cart would give them a better idea as to how the lighter one would go. David would help to push it and guide it through the current if it did not touch bottom and lost traction.

Now it was a matter of time before they knew if David's plan would work. But the tide moves slowly when you are watching and waiting, so once everything was prepared, they sat down for a while to enjoy the waves rolling in. Alicia went looking for shells that were plentiful with no one to ever collect them now, while David checked the ropes and the loads on the carts over and over to reassure himself and to bleed off tension and nervous energy.

As they were preparing the first crossing and waiting for the tide to go out, David noticed and pointed out to Alicia that the tide had gone down significantly and that the flow over the sand bar seemed more shallow. The current in what was the deepest part that had gone to David's chest in the past seemed safer as well.

"Do I hear thunder again?"

"Yes, David, and look up there," Alicia said with a sense of foreboding in her voice.

Looking inland toward the mountain where she pointed, David saw a huge, black late-afternoon storm cloud that had built up and was pouring rain not more than twenty miles away. His fear was that it could produce a flash flood.

He did not want to worry Alicia, but what he saw produced a fear that got his heart pumping with the adrenaline again that came naturally in humans in response to danger. "Uh-oh," he murmured in the calmest voice he could muster. "We had better get moving. That storm is dumping a whole lot of water that's eventually going to flow down the stream into this river and pass right by here on its way to the ocean."

He was on target to fear the oncoming water. Flash-flooding along rivers coming out of the mountains and washing out bridges and buildings was common.

Quickly, Alicia moved her vehicle out into the water. The length of the cart seemed to give it less traction, and it appeared to creep across the mixed sandy and rocky river bottom. Approaching the deepest and swiftest part of the current, the rear end began to lose contact with the river bed and swing toward the sea.

"David," Alicia's voice cried out. "I'm losing it."

"No, you aren't," David replied. "It's a little wobbly but just keep moving it on. I'm able to push down on it, adding a little weight and it is catching the river bottom from time to time. Keep on and I think we will be past it in just a few minutes."

His unending optimism annoyed Alicia right now. She was more cautious and much less of a risk taker and he would prod her to do things that she was not sure were so wise. This was another of those times.

She too had had her experiences through the years that gave her a healthy respect for certain situations. Too close for comfort to drowning while holding one of their children in an ocean with a strong undertow was one such experience. The thought that she could not keep her child above water and would also drown went through her head about the instant that she felt sand. Digging in as deep as she could and using what she was sure was her only chance, she pushed off as the next wave floated her and their child to safety. A lifeguard, ill-equipped to handle the ocean waves, she knew that it was God-given timing that brought her to safety. She sat just watching the water and thanking God that she and their daughter had not drowned.

That was years ago, but it was fresh enough to cause her heart to skip a beat when she thought about the details of that day.

She was not interested in another close encounter with drowning. They had experienced one to many near misses just today.

"This is not worth the risk David!" she shouted. She could feel the drag of the current toward the ocean and was almost paralyzed by her fear. Her heart pounding, eyes wide open, frozen in place and taking rapid breaths, she could hardly move.

Knowing what was happening, David yelled out, hoping to break through her fear that she had to move forward because there was no way to turn back.

David kept talking to her in a reassuring voice, encouraging her along, and Alicia did as he said, as she did each other time when she was in a dangerous situation. Within a few minutes the vehicle was past the dangerous point and moving steadily on shore. She was sure that she struggled for 30 minutes, but it wasn't. With tension so great, every muscle in her body was taut.

"Pull it up away from the river as far as you can go along the beach—away from any flood zone," David called to her. "I'm heading back for the other one."

"Be careful, David. That storm is getting closer and the rain is pouring up in the mountain. It is only going to get deeper. Please hurry!" she added with strain in her voice as he crossed back for the other cart.

"What are we doing?" Or more, *"Why are we doing it? I've about had it with all of this!*

He grasped the line for safety to make it to the other side as quickly as possible. Time was ticking away for them to get this part of the trip over with. He wanted as much as Alicia to be standing next to her with the carts and goods on higher ground when the stream began to rise from the deluge.

"Ok, Hon, I'll be right back." David plunged back into the moving stream and pulled himself across with the rope that he had stretched from one side to the other.

But when he got to the other side, he took off in the opposite direction, away from the cart. She yelled to him, but he did not answer.

She could not believe he was going someplace and not crossing immediately. What was he thinking? "What could possibly be so important that he would not get across now?" she muttered under her breath,

Then she realized he had changed a battery up near the jungle shade. She knew they could not leave it in the elements, and also they would not make it back to San Juan without the full sets of batteries. She saw him moving quickly toward the spot where the battery would be and return with it. Every second was counting at this point as the storm continued upstream.

The battery would add weight to the cart as well, when every little bit helped to anchor the wheels on the sandbar. It was already iffy that the lighter cart could make it across.

Though the tide had continued to go out some more, the river seemed to have risen in just the time that it took them to get the first vehicle safely past the rushing water, and now even more with the minutes lost going back for the battery.

Quickly mounting the smaller vehicle, David geared up and drove into the river. At first the car moved along with little resistance, but with the rising water and increasingly swift current, David began to have serious doubts himself.

New currents pushed the golf-cart as the storm hit where they were. Wind and rain poured down at the cart and David as the current relentlessly tried to move them off course. The shorter vehicle seemed a little easier to control, but then the back swung out just as Alicia's had, only there was no one there to add extra weight.

David quickly reached back for his heavy tool box that he had received as a gift their first Christmas together. Pushing it down against the accelerator, it kept the vehicle's wheels turning. David jumped over the seat into the back and then leaned over the seats to steer the vehicle while adding more weight to the rear section.

Those additional pounds seemed to give enough additional traction as the cart again touched bottom and began to move ahead in a cockeyed direction similar to a sand crab walking down the beach.

"Come on baby, move," David whispered under his breath. Finally, agonizingly slowly, the vehicle steadied and moved ahead, passing out of the deepening current.

The rain continued to pelt the vehicle as Alicia, who had been waiting beside the rushing water, jumped in beside him and they rode on out of the river bed onto the beach and away from the rising water.

It took a while for them both to recuperate from the overwhelming tension that had overtaken them again this time. They just stood close to each other for several minutes and watched as the water rushed past them and the tension washed away.

They stood dripping wet as they continued to be pelted by the tropical warm rain and wind.

"Whew," he exclaimed "That sure was close."

"Yes. I just might stay on this side and never go across again, especially if it is like this on the way back," Alicia said, touching his arm gently. "I'm just glad that we are safe and got across the river."

"Me too," David said with a nervous grin that Alicia had grown to know. "Now, let's find some place to get out of the storm and spend the night. I know it is early, but we have both had enough for a day, yes?"

"No trouble agreeing with you there," came the emphatic response.

They immediately changed out of their wet clothes with the storm mostly past and into something dry, knowing that even in the jungle there could be a chill in the air.

When they did find a place, the sky had grown very dark with the storm clouds as well as the declining sunlight as night approached. Making their way through an old, very overgrown path to the highway, they spied an old store and garage about a quarter of a mile away.

"Look, a building with no obstacles between here and there. Wow. How nice," Alicia pointed out with obvious relief very apparent in her voice.

"Right," he agreed. "Even with the scorpions and overgrown roof, it will be home sweet home for tonight!"

"Oh, please! Let's not talk about the scorpions. At least it will offer shelter. Even if it is musty, it is a roof over our heads to protect against any other storms that pop up during the night."

As they got closer they realized it was like the shelter of any gas station with lots of clear area under a protective roof. There were a few areas that were damaged and offered no protection, but plenty of area that did. They would not have to go in the building, and yet be protected. They were almost excited about their 'luxury accommodation'.

As they set up, the sky cleared as it often did in the tropics after a strong storm and they discussed the day and what went well and what did not, both trying to dwell on the good, not the horrible of the day. After a meal they drifted off to sleep listening to what they assumed were mice scurrying near them as well as to the jungle sounds as darkness brought out the nocturnal animals.

An early start took them the rest of the way to their destination. Alicia's dream of a rest in one of the most beautiful spots in Costa Brava was finally fulfilled. After the experiences of yesterday, they needed rest more than ever.

Chapter 18

Their ride into the hippy, coastal village that had always been on a narrow two lane dirt road and a challenge before "the event" was even more so now. Mud and puddles up to their hubcaps on their old Trooper had always caused them to move slowly and to rock back and forth as they dropped into the muddy potholes. But this trip it was even more challenging. The tire indentations were still there. But the carts were lower than a car or their Trooper. Slow progress achieved their goal even though they touched bottom many times and rocked back and forth into and out of the mud potholes.

Using the machete to clear the path was becoming more and more expected. After the event that took humanity, most growth was the vegetation on the ground. The many species of plants and trees remained as they were. The couple was always amazed at how nature could mend itself when man stayed out of the natural process.

They were delighted to find upon arrival at the village that their favorite Hotel, *Cabinas Toucan*, had not totally collapsed.

In fact, Alicia smiled with satisfaction as she explored the restaurant kitchen area and found that, though it was full of vines, dirty and needed cleaning, it was usable for heating up their food. The gas burners even worked with the light of a match, much to her surprise. The tanks were full.

She set to work to clean up only what was necessary to make it acceptable to her. The huge veranda with swings and hammocks hanging from the heavy cross beams, tables where breakfast was served when there were guests were still there. And, even the ping-pong table was in its usual place and usable, if they could find where the owner stored the paddles at night to keep them from "walking".

The cabin opened on three sides to the air, with a rustic ceiling of bamboo. The setting was a park-like ground that had become overgrown with plants and with vines that had grown up through the cracks in the floor. They were able to clear and clean space in about a half-day.

The gruesome job of hauling away several skeletons was the most unpleasant part of the whole cleaning up process, and one that they would never adjust to. It was simply a job that had to be done.

They explored the row of cottages closest to the ocean and set up home in one of the ocean-front rooms. David was able to find a stream that ended not too far from their cabin and the veranda, and he hauled water for bathing and food preparation.

The cottages were originally built with screens to let the tropical sea-breezes through, so they were able to open the shutters on one of the cabins and enjoy fresh air and the smells of tropical flowers and fruits. Cabins that were in the back of the property had been used for storage and had started to deteriorate badly when they were last there 'ages ago'.

Now they were hardly visible and not worth even exploring. Again, their own fresh sheets and a blanket made the room comfortable enough. And by this time they had both accustomed themselves to a rustic life style when not at home in their apartment in the city.

That evening the couple went down to Black Beach. Just as the name indicated, the sand was black as slate. What a contrast to the white sugar beaches of the coastal route they had seen.

The sight brought back memories of previous trips to this favorite spot, and they found a comfortable place to sit on the beach to watch the water until it was too dark to see. With the help of a light, they went back and fell asleep against the night sounds of the jungle.

The next morning brought back more vivid memories to both of them. Before the first light of dawn, the howler monkeys began their loud deep calls, waking Alicia who had always been a light sleeper. They seemed to be talking to each other with the original call and a less audible response in the distance. As she lay still they seemed to get closer. She remembered these from every other times they had been to Langosta, and it was never clear as to why they started so early in the morning. By nine in the morning they were quiet or gone. Though they could see the leaves on the trees moving indicating the monkeys were there, except on the beach where they could see several other types of monkeys, they never actually saw the howlers.

Later they would see Toucans and other birds, raccoons, lizards and occasionally snakes. But the monkeys were always the most interesting to the couple.

As she lay still listening to the monkeys, she thought of the uniqueness of this area of Costa Brava. Though thick with vegetation in the city where they lived, at the beach the biodiversity was so different. The change had always been nice, and this time was no exception. Such beautiful palms, flowering trees and wild fruits.

The famous Playa Langosta National Park was a few miles away but they were able to go back and forth each day by commandeering some bicycles that they found in a rental store that had always been just next door to the hotel. A little oil and grease found at the bike shop and pumping up of the tires with a portable hand pump had them on the road within twenty-four hours after their arrival. Whatever the weather, they made the trip back and forth each day during what turned out to be a wonderful stay on the beautiful coast.

The park's beach, lined with palms and other species, offered shade along the edge of the white sand beach. A half-hour from the cabin they sat in a wide space in shade where they could relax and watch the water change color as the sun moved overhead and to the west. By three o'clock each afternoon they were ready for the half-hour ride back to the hotel where they cooked, then sat on the hanging nylon hammocks or swinging chairs and read or talked.

"David," Alicia called out to him as he was reading one afternoon.

"Yes, what's up?"

"David, I was just wondering if you remember the last time we were here."

"Of course I do," he responded. "Let's see, it was about a year before 'the incident' when the kids were here, right?"

"Right," she responded. "That was the last time we saw them you know." She quietly began to tear up as she thought about the long separation from their children and the uncertainty over knowing their fate. They were certain that they had died with all others and were mere skeletons someplace. They had talked about it from time to time since that unusual day, and it never got any easier for them. They always came to the same ending—that they would never know.

They hadn't mentioned the children too often because the subject was too painful for them to consider. Even though separated by so many miles, they had remained close to both Rich and Melanie and their families.

Rich had gone to college in Florida and then joined a major Christian NGO that built housing for the poor around the world. He had been assigned to El Salvador for several years before their last visit and enjoyed the expat life as much as his parents did.

In college he had met Meg, his wife, and they had fallen in love almost at first sight. She, too, had grown up overseas, the daughter of missionary parents in the Philippines. As a result, she too was a third-culture kid and had so much in common with Rich.

Soon after their marriage, their first assignment was to Peru where both of their children were born and attended an English-language international school. Eventually, the NGO promoted Rich to country director and transferred them to El Salvador where he presided over an ever-expanding program of house construction.

Melanie, on the other hand, had waited quite some time to get married. She earned a degree in international business at a Christian school in Kentucky and quickly got on with an import-export business in Fort Lauderdale. For the first five years after graduation she was busy building her career while completing a master's degree. In between classes she traveled throughout the Americas which was how she had been able to visit David and Alicia frequently.

On one such trip she met Carlos, an Argentinian diplomat who traveled often to Miami. Between their frequent business trips, they were able to maintain a friendship that slowly developed into something more. Finally, using family connections, he was able to snag a position at the Argentinian consulate in Miami and their relationship grew from there. They had married about three years earlier when the family was last together at Langosta.

David reached over and touched Alicia's arm. "It's been tough in that regard, hasn't it, Hon?" he asked gently.

"Yes, it has," she said between quiet sniffles. "And not knowing what happened to them has always been more difficult than knowing for sure."

Brightening a bit, she continued, "But you know, as difficult and bizarre as these last years have been, they haven't been all bad."

"Really?" David said. "Do you really think that?"

"Yes, I really do," she said after some thought. "After all, we city folk have been able to carve out a life and survive quite comfortably during this time. We've lived with many of the amenities of life we had before, and we've have eaten well. We haven't had any major illnesses; our injuries have been of the cuts and bruises type, we haven't had any communicable diseases because there hasn't been anybody around to transmit them to us. We have learned to entertain ourselves through videos at first and books, board games, and adventures away from home—thanks to your genius at setting up solar power and other ways of doing things. Yes, I think we have done quite well in spite of the terrible loneliness and not knowing what happened to the kids."

David smiled and reflected in silence for a few minutes. "You know, you are right. I guess that some days we, or at least I, get so involved in the day-to-day survival and getting everything done that I don't take enough time to reflect or give thanks for what we have had and how we have survived. Yet, we have always had enough to eat, we have been able to keep up the house...or houses...depending on how you want to look at it, and, as you said, we have stayed heathy. We traded our work that was always the center of our life for survival, and maybe that is not all bad.

"Not only that," Alicia added, "We have continued to have some exotic adventures like this crazy trip to Langosta."

The comment brought a chuckle for a minute, and they grew silent, likely each thinking of the river crossing.

"Not only that," Alicia continued. "We have had each other and that has made it possible and good."

David leaned over and kissed her. "You're right, Hon. That has been the best part."

After a short pause, she giggled and added, "I am sure glad we like each other." That caused them both to laugh.

They sat for a while enjoying the sound of the waves breaking on the shore and the occasional howl of an animal or a sound distinct to a jungle bird coming from somewhere back in the forests.

"I suppose that at times the enormity of the whole thing has overwhelmed you like it has me," David said, again breaking into Alicia's thoughts.

"Yes," Alicia responded slowly. "At times the separation from the children and the uncertainty has kept me awake some nights. And, the loss of so many precious friendships and the inability to escape from where we were," she added trailing off.

They both reflected for a few moments. Alicia continued, "But what has left me perplexed so often are the unanswered questions. I know we have talked about it before, but…"and she trailed off for a few seconds.

David grunted in agreement.

And she began again the conversation so familiar to them both, "Like, how did this all happen and why did it happen and why are we the only people in San Juan and perhaps the whole country and even the whole world who are still alive? Those are questions that obviously I'll never answer, but I sure would like to know."

"I know what you mean," David mused. "I cannot fathom what caused the massive deaths of millions, billions, of people. So many things that you could guess couldn't have been the cause or we would have died too. A global chemical exposure, a massive epidemic, a radiation attack," and he let out a brief laugh here for a moment, "a bizarre attack from little men from Mars… None of them could have done it or we would have succumbed too."

"Or," Alicia interjected, "for some totally unexplainable reason we were immune to whatever took everybody else. Maybe we have a specific gene."

"Yeah, maybe…" David said. "But that seems very improbable since we are from two different sets of genes.

"Yes, I know, but…." Alicia pondered for a moment. "But…if we were immune to such an attack, because the immunity was hereditary, the kids could have survived after all."

David remained silent and then turned to Alicia. Seeing the fleeting moment of hope on her face, he said, "Yeah, hereditary. Genes. Maybe that's what happened." David really did not believe they had survived for that reason, but he did not want to dash what hope Alicia had.

Finally, David and Alicia knew they needed to head back to the city. They would gladly have stayed longer, but realized they faced gardens that needed tending and property that would need attention. And the reality of the trip back was also part of the mix. Going back meant streams and a river to ford again, chances of a break down and numerous other things to think about.

Though they were dreading the return trip, they knew they could not stay at their dream location forever.

The night before they left as they were taking in the wonderful tropical breezes, enjoying the afternoon shower, walking the beach in the national park for the last time, David turned to Alicia, "Do you remember how many times I said if I ever disappeared, check down at Langosta Beach?"

"Absolutely! It has a whole new meaning now, doesn't it?" she responded with a little laugh.

"Funny you said that. I was thinking the same thing."

The next morning they started out at first light they packed a quick breakfast which they would eat as they headed up the way. They both realized that they very likely would never be back again. As they packed the carts there was sadness in them but also a feeling of refreshment which helped to neutralize other feelings and emotions. But the most prominent was satisfaction and contentment.

Going back they knew much better what to expect. They knew the way was cleared and that places to stop and stay overnight would need little preparation as they had on the way down. Only the place they had stayed after they had crossed the river would have to be replaced by a new shelter because they fully expected to get further than the shelter of the gas station the first night.

After loading their final supplies into the carts, they got a mid-morning start. Wistfully saying good-bye to the hotel as if it was an animate object they started their journey back. Both had tears in their eyes as they pulled away.

Compared to the way down, the trip was easy and they arrived refreshed and ready to tackle the gardening and other survival tasks they had left for a while.

Chapter 19

Ten years later.

David and Alicia prided themselves with their good health since "the incident." Even before their lives radically changed they had suffered nothing more serious than the usual colds and bouts of the flu. They had exercised daily, sometimes in a nearby gym, more often by walking the tree-lined neighborhood in which they lived.

And, prior to the change, like many expatriates, they found themselves walking much more than they would have back home in the States. The low cost and efficiency of bus systems had found them using public transportation for many trips. Those, of course, meant that they would walk up hill a few blocks to the bus stop and then a few more blocks from the end of the bus line to their offices at the university.

In addition, they frequently had walked to the *MegaBodega* store as well as for small purchases at the neighborhood mall just four or five blocks in a different direction from the bus stop. The nightly walk gave them the opportunity to stretch their legs after sitting behind a desk or being on their feet all day teaching, as well as a chance to enjoy the cool air of the evening.

After they began life on their own, the daily ritual of survival assured that they exercised whether they wanted to or not. Those days were, however, very routine. Even as they worked to connect solar power to the apartment building or searched the neighborhood for what they needed, they exercised a lot. The patterns changed again after their car could no longer be used as gasoline deteriorated.

They gave up hope of other human contact, including seeing their kids and grandchildren. As the surroundings became more and more uninhabitable birds and other native animals became prolific. Rivers were no longer polluted; trash which had once littered the streets had finally decomposed completely.

Gardening, preparing food and maintaining the buildings meant that they were on their feet most of the day from sunrise to late afternoon or after sunset. That active life played a major role in their longevity and protection from the decline of physical functions later in life.

Of course, they had aged and lost some weight with not eating out in restaurants and not having access to so many sweet products or impulsive purchases of items such as ice cream. And, as they aged, their hair turned grey and they noticed more wrinkles as well as changes to their skin as they looked in the mirror. They took on other characteristics that came with that process of time.

But, as they reached their mid-seventies, that vitality and healthy regimen began to fail. It was a little more difficult for each of them to keep up, so anything not absolutely necessary went by the wayside. That gave them a chance to sneak in an afternoon nap that was impossible for many years.

For a year or more, David noticed that Alicia seemed to slow down markedly. Often she was short of breath after climbing the stairs. Her stamina had waned and he found himself stepping in more and more to assume responsibilities that she had carried for so many years.

He would frequently ask, "Are you ok?"

And her response in a tentative voice was always, "Yes." But he was never totally certain it was a straight forward and honest answer.

Soon, he was washing the dishes by himself after each meal and spending more time cleaning the house, and, he was keeping up with the activities she had always handled.

He encouraged her to rest more frequently and he found himself spending less time in the gardens…just enough to survive.

He too had to admit he did not have the energy of his mid-life years and had slowed down in recent years. No longer could he work the long hours in the hot sun. The energy to dig and hoe and weed was waning in him.

For several years he had been unable and, to be truthful, unwilling to climb up on the roof to repair leaks. For that reason, several wet spots had appeared throughout their apartment and they solved the problem now by placing buckets under the drips.

In addition, he no longer cut the lawn frequently and he had long ago given upon keeping neighboring lawns trimmed and cleaned.

In fact, survival, which had been at the center of their activities for years, now had become so much more difficult and, perhaps, almost impossible.

By mid to late afternoon, when the rains came and the lightening flashed and the thunder rolled over the central valley, David and Alicia often found themselves sitting on the couch looking out over the vista that they had seen thousands of times.

David spent numerous hours and sleepless nights worrying about what would happen to either of them if the other became unable to function at all. He wondered how they would eat or maintain themselves if he were to become incapacitated now that Alicia was able to do less and less. And, he worried about how either one of them would survive, physically or emotionally if, or more accurately, when the other one died.

Certainly their diet was suffering. No longer able to grow such an abundant garden, even in the rich tropical climate, and not having the large reserve of canned food that Alicia prepared every year, they found themselves eating less and less, using only what they could immediately harvest day by day.

David was still able to capture an animal from time to time which provided some of the protein that they required. But, he found his hunting skills waning and his stamina to forage for meat lacking. The cows had run wild years ago.

Now, the situation seemed to be reaching a crisis point. It appeared to David that Alicia might have suffered a slight stroke. Her speech was slightly slurred, her walking became erratic and her ability even to heat water or cook the simplest meal was limited.

David stepped in the best he could, but was also certain that their failing diet was contributing to their physical decline. He struggled with each month to get to the gardens to look for fresh fruit and vegetables and put them together into some type of meal. He missed Alecia's good cooking, but did the best he knew how.

Washing clothes, which was very much a physical job, completely wore him out. He labored to get Alicia up each morning and help her get dressed, then feed and care for her while also going out for food or looking for other supplies. He was certain that she was not in pain or noticeably suffering from her infirmities, for which he was grateful, but he was unable to know how to prevent her continued deterioration.

Finally, he began to contemplate what might be the end. All along they had faced the reality that when they could no longer function, there would be nobody to take care of them, no retirement home to which they could go, no medical or hospice care to assist them in their final days.

And, there would be no one else to either mourn them or pick up where they left off. They would be the last.

David had not been considering these issues in depth for long before the day came when Alicia could not get up from the bed. It seemed that she had suffered another attack and had lost the ability and, perhaps the will, to do much more than lie in bed staring at the ceiling.

When David sat by her, she would hold his hand and close her eyes. It was obvious to David that she was at peace and comfortable in spite of her situation. Now, he spent every possible hour with her, leaving only to seek out and prepare a meager meal or get some water. At night he would lie alongside her, listening to her faint breathing and pray that at least she would not suffer.

Then, after just a few days, he noticed that as he sat holding her hand, massaging her arms, her breathing became labored and, shortly thereafter, it stopped.

David squeezed her hand, and he cried, knowing the end had come for her. Not having her alive and by his side was unbearable. Being alone was almost too much for him. His will and reason to live was gone.

Chapter 20

After an hour or so, David slowly got up and walked to the living room. Standing by the large double window, he looked out over the scene that they had shared together thousands of times over the past decades.

As his eyes moved up along the mountain ridges, he remembered the times that they had traveled the back roads and hiked along the trails of this beautiful country. Looking down below, he thought about their various errands throughout the city, especially in the early years of their solo life together in this tropical paradise.

And, he remembered the countless evenings when, after difficult, demanding, physically tiring days, they would sit in the semi-darkness, together, watching the last light of the sun's rays bounce off of the mountainsides and the nearer buildings of the city as they talked, shared their emotions, joys and frustrations, their insights and ideas as well as their love for each other.

Oh how he loved this small country and the time they had spent in Costa Brava.

Now, another night was falling, but this one so different than those that had passed before. There was no one with whom he could share his thoughts, his feelings, his love. The silence, the loneliness, the uncertainty, the fear overwhelmed him, and he broke into sobs that only he could hear.

Slowly, he turned and walked back to the bedroom. Drawing aside the bed covers, he lay down next to Alicia and tried to sleep.

As the sun came up over the Izkatzu volcano, David was already up and out of the house. Sleep at best had been intermittent and there seemed to be an urgency about his morning activities.

Picking up several shovels from the garage, he slowly made his way down the block and across the street to the small park-like setting they had maintained throughout the years. Here, many years ago, the couple had placed a park bench overlooking the deep ravine down to the river that ran below their street. This patch was one area that David had kept mowed, trimmed and planted with the flowering tropical plants that they both enjoyed.

Here, when time and chores permitted, they had often passed thirty minutes in the late afternoon watching the humming birds flit back and forth between the richly-colored tropical blooms while the black hawks screeched and flew overhead. They amused themselves watching the voracious cutter ants as they carried huge chewed-off pieces of leaves along their well-worn paths to their lair. From here, they saw the occasional squirrel and deer which roamed the neighborhoods. It was their place of respite before going back to the apartment where dinner needed to be prepared and consumed and other chores done before they could again relax together, enjoying the view through their huge front windows.

David didn't stop this morning to enjoy the flora nor fauna. He had a task that he had to do.

Stepping out in front of the bench where they had passed those late afternoons, David pushed the spade into the ground and began to dig.

It was here that the infirmities of his age began to show even more. Only a few shovels left him winded and made his muscles ache. He dug, but found himself having to stop frequently to catch his breath and gather up the strength to continue with the task.

Persistently, he dug however. He wasn't concerned about depth—he only needed enough space to meet the need. Slowly the large hole took shape as a mound of freshly dug soil piled up alongside.

After several hours, he was satisfied. "This will do," he said, as if talking to Alicia.

Now came the hard part, both physically and emotionally.

Leaving the shovels by the side of the freshly-dug hole, David returned to the apartment. Slowly climbing the stairs, having to stop repeatedly to catch his breath, he reached their apartment that had been their home since coming to Costa Brava years ago.

David stepped inside. Instinctively he called, "Alicia." Immediately he realized what he had done and his emotions collapsed. Tears washed down his face as he went back to their bedroom. There, Alicia's body lay, sweet and peaceful, just as he had left her.

Exhausted, he sat beside her on the bed. Again taking her cold hand, he brushed the hair from her forehead and leaned over to kiss her. It must have been his imagination, but he was almost certain that she smiled as he did so.

Rising, he went to the closet and pulled out a few blankets. "I'll be right back, Hon," he called as he walked out the door and back to the hole he had dug.

Lining the hole with the blankets, and satisfied with his work, he returned to the apartment.

"It's time to go, Hon," he called as he entered the bedroom.

There was a time when he could easily lift and carry her. After all, he had carried her across the threshold of their first apartment after their marriage, hadn't he? He could do it again, he was sure.

Slowly, ever-so-slowly, he carried her down the stairs and placed her in the wagon that he had positioned right outside the gate.

Pulling her, like a little boy would pull his childhood girlfriend in a wagon, David guided it across the street to their own private park. There, he struggled to lift her and slowly, almost reverently, placed her body on one of the blankets he had spread out in the hole.

Pulling another blanket over her, he bent down and kissed her on the cheek. Straightening up, he used one of the shovels to cover her body and protect her, as he always had, from any harm that might come her way.

Kneeling down beside her grave, he offered a prayer, giving thanks for her, for their lives together, and for their love.

Rising up, he moved to the other side of the hole where he had excavated more dirt. There, he had also placed another blanket.

Almost at the point of collapse, David lay down and pulled the last blanket he had there over himself. Now, he was at peace beside his beloved Alicia.

David closed his eyes and fell silent.

Epilogue

As David's breathing ceased, the great black hawk that had been sitting high up in a nearby tree for most of the morning gave forth a mighty screech and, spreading its huge wings, lifted up into the sky.

Slowly circling as it rose higher, the bird made several passes over David and Alicia's park, then turned and flew off as with a mission to the northeast, its powerful wings propelling it ever so much higher and increasing its speed as it moved away from the usual haunts over the ravine and the river below.

Soaring on the ever-present wind current, the giant bird flew with intensity over the river, past the deteriorated government hospital along the *autopista*. Then turning and following the Pan-American Highway, it flew without ceasing for nearly fifteen miles.

Where the highway crested a low-lying hill, offering anyone who entered the city their first glimpse of the metropolitan area, the bird slowed its pace and began to circle down toward a clump of trees.

As it descended, it again uttered its distinctive cry as, exhausted, it settled on to a limb that stretched out toward the highway.

"Look at that Rich," exclaimed the 55-ish man standing with a group of others surveying the scene spread out before them. "That's one of the biggest black hawks I have ever seen."

"You're right," Rich replied, eyeing the big bird that appeared to be on the brink of collapse. "And look at him; he looks like he has flown beyond his usual range. See how he seems to be just plain worn out?"

"Yeah, he does," the other man said. "I wonder what's up. Perhaps he was frightened by some predator and decided that getting a good distance away was his best option."

"Maybe you are right," Rich acknowledged. "There used to be hawks that circled above the river at the bottom of the ravine below where my folks lived," he remembered. "But, I don't recall them being that big. Maybe living without competition from human threats has allowed that species to grow and prosper. Who knows?"

The two men remained silent for a while. Then the other spoke. "Speaking of your parents, do you suppose you remember where they lived?"

"Oh, sure. I was here many times when they were teaching at the "U", Rich replied. "It's not hard to find. The issue, of course, as with this whole trip, is whether we can get through the streets and the debris and the earthquake and flood damage to get there."

"And if they still live there at that place--if they survived at all," said the first.

"Well, Rich, you know that if we have been able to circumvent all of the obstacles we have encountered in the past three months between El

Salvador and here, certainly we can negotiate the last few miles and check it out."

"Yeah, you're right," Rich said. "But, there's no rush, really. Remember, as I told you, they would be in their late 70s by now, assuming that they or anyone survived here in Costa Brava. I'm afraid the odds on that aren't very high."

"Yeah, but you never know," his friend replied. "If I were a betting man, I would wager that they didn't survive, just like everyone else. Just look out at this valley—a whole city of nearly a million people and there is no sign of any life. No smoke, no open areas, just old buildings overgrown by decades of tropical growth and crumbling just like most of the buildings in San Salvador and the other cities we have passed through."

"You know," Rich mused. "Since we decided to launch out like early explorers who set out from Spain, England or Portugal to discover the New World we have not run across one other human being in any city or small town or community through which we have passed?"

"It seems to me that if the half-dozen or so of us who we are certain survived in El Salvador made it through whatever it was that happened, there should be at least a few in each city or at least country where we passed. Don't you agree?"

"Right again," his friend replied. "But, we pretty-well scoured most of Managua, riding up and down any passable streets, walking through communities, taking a broad perspective from the top floor of that old pyramid-shaped hotel, and we didn't see any sign of human life. No smoke, no cleared areas for farming or gardening, no kept-up yards and houses as we have done in Salvador. There just wasn't any sign of human life anywhere. Just skeletons and lots of jungle."

"Yes, lots of skeletons."

"So, then, why would we think that there might be any survivors, including my parents, here?" Rich asked, continuing the exchange. "Logic tells me that they died just like anyone else and there is a possibility that there is no one else alive in this city either."

The two men stood silently for a few moments, each deep in their thoughts as they scanned the large central valley of Costa Brava one more time with binoculars. To the east they could see a wisp of smoke from Izkatzu floating above the mountain. Around them they could hear the call of birds and the distant growl of the omnipresent howler monkeys. A light breeze moved the leaves on the trees and bushes around them.

Then one of the men settled the binoculars on a patch way off in the distance that looked a little different…not overgrown like other parts of the city. That was a little odd, but it was not the first strange thing they had seen on this trip.

"Well, I guess we ought to push on," the other man said.

Rich nodded in agreement as they turned and headed back to the large solar-powered vehicles behind them where their wives and other family members awaited them.

"Did you see anything Rich?" asked Meg, his wife, from the passenger seat.

"No, Hon, nothing, j.ust as I thought. But, we're here, so let's get moving."

Rich jumped into the driver's seat and led the convoy of vehicles on toward the capitol city of Costa Brava.

As they began the last few miles of their journey, the huge black hawk let out another ear-piercing screech and lifted off of the branch.

Catching the warm air currents, he circled higher above them and then, screeching again, set out ahead, more slowly, circling back from time to time as if not to get too far ahead of them, then moving on, heading in the direction from which he had come, back toward his home on the banks of the ravine above the river.

Questions:

If you were stranded someplace with no other human life, where would you like to be? Why?

What do you think caused most everyone to die?

What would you have done differently if you had been in David's or Alicia's place?

What are some things that the author did not include in this book that you think you might encounter?

If you were to write a sequel to this book, how would you develop it?

Made in United States
Orlando, FL
26 November 2023